CW00520341

IMAGINATION 2

PAUL LUDFORD

T: 07519 746 963
F: Thenovelistpl
E: paul@paulludford.com

Author of Novels and Short Stories

www.paulludford.com

PAUL LUDFORD is now retired, having spent time as an apprentice cutter in a corset factory, waited at tables on an ocean-going mail/passenger ship, operated printing presses, and worked his way up to management level in an international insurance company. Not content with taking life easy after early retirement, he spent two seasons caring for two charter cruisers operating on the Solent in the South of England. He also spent several happy years meeting people and listening to their stories as he drove a bus between Portsmouth and Brighton, probably his most enjoyable paid occupation.

Having discovered the joy of writing, he now spends many happy hours on the keyboard using his imagination as he invents his characters and creates their stories.

First published 2023

Copyright - Paul Ludford 2023

ISBN 978-1-915787-58-3

The right of Paul Ludford to be identified as

The author of this work has been asserted by him

In accordance with the Copyright, Designs and Patent

Act 1988

Printed in Great Britain by

Biddles Books Limited, King's Lynn, Norfolk

CONTENTS

The Saucepan

'This is so stupid, why did I ever agree to your idea of playing a game of "Doctor Who?" Why not a simple game of "Hide and Seek" or "Hop-Scotch?" Oh no, you wanted "Doctor Who." And why the saucepan? I mean, who wants to go around with a saucepan on their head, that's what I want to know?' Frank Bennet's mother was in a state. Her plans for today certainly had not included a bus ride to the fire station where she hoped the saucepan would be eased off without the risk of an ear being ripped off along with it.

'You have to use a saucepan when you're a Dalek, Mum,' explained the boy. 'The handle is the death ray. **Annihilate!!!!'**

'Will you stop saying that, Frank? It's beginning to get on my nerves,' retorted Mrs Bennet as she checked her appearance in the hall mirror.

'**Exterminate, exterminate!!!'**

'Nor that. Just keep quiet, and let me think.'

'I am a Dalek, I am a Dalek, I am ...'

'Frank!'

'Will the firemen be able to get the saucepan off, Mum? I tried ever so hard, and so did you. It didn't move, did it?'

'I'm sure they will, they have all sorts of equipment for things like this. Remember when your friend Sid got his knee stuck in the railings at the park, and how they managed to bend the bar with a long metal thing?'

'That's cool, Mum. Do you think they'll have to cut the saucepan off with a torch thing, like they do with crashed cars on the telly?'

'No Frank, they won't do that. Now get your coat on, the bus will be along in ten minutes, if it's on time for a change.'

Five minutes later, mother, son and saucepan were hurrying along the pavement toward the bus stop when they unfortunately bumped into Mrs Flint. The elderly lady immediately ceased her task of heaving her dustbin out to the front gate in order to peer over her spectacles at her two neighbours.

‘Oh, it’s Mrs Bennet,’ said she, after a close inspection. ‘I don’t see so well these days you know. Oh, and it’s little Frankie. Be a love and help me move this bin, there’s a dear.’

‘I am a Dalek; I am a Dalek.’

‘What’s that, dear?’

‘Exterminate!!!!’

‘Frank! I’ve told you to stop that nonsense! I’m sorry Mrs Flint, only we must go; we need to catch the bus to the fire station.’

‘Oh dear! Is there a fire somewhere?’ replied Mrs Flint in sudden alarm. ‘I expect it was those fireworks I heard last night. It should not be allowed.’

‘No, Mrs Flint. There is no fire. We must go and get this saucepan removed, that’s all.’

‘Oh, is that what it is? I did not want to say anything in case my poor old eyes were playing tricks on me again. Do you know, the other day I thought I saw a dog smoking a pipe? It turned out to be a telephone repair man sitting on the edge of his manhole having a rest. Did I ever tell you about the time my Bert got his big toe stuck up the cold-water tap? He needed me to help him, poor dear. He was so embarrassed because I had never seen him completely … you know. Always had at least his socks on. I had never seen anything …'

'Come on Frank! We'll miss that bus if we don't get a move on. Bye, Mrs Flint.'

'Oh … bye-bye then.'

Turning the corner, they were just in time to see the back of the bus as it pulled away from the stop.

'I knew it! This day will get worse before it gets better, or my name isn't June Bennet. Fifteen minutes we'll have to wait, and don't you dare start your Dalek nonsense again. Just wait till your father gets home. He'll be expecting a stew in that saucepan, not a head.'

'Excuse me, madam, was that the number six by any chance?' This from a well-dressed gentleman. He was gazing at the saucepan as he addressed the boy's mother.

'Yes, it was, we just missed it. Sorry.'

'Oh well, never mind. That looks painful. It is a saucepan I assume?'

'No, it's the top of a Dalek, isn't that obvious?' retorted an extremely frustrated mother.

'Well, now you mention it, I suppose it is. Exterminate and that sort of thing.'

'Exterminate! ... exterminate! ... I am a Dalek.'

'Now you've set him off again. That's *enough,* Frank. It's not funny anymore.'

'He sounds very scary, doesn't he?' said the gentleman with a smile. 'I remember the time when my son swallowed a whistle. They said it would come out naturally, but two days later, whenever he had flatulence, he sounded like a soccer referee! We had to put up with that for a whole day. Never did use that whistle again. Ah, here's our bus, the one we missed must have been running late, or this one's early. Well best of luck with the saucepan.'

The bus pulled into the bay with a loud hiss from its brakes. The door opened with a swish and a clatter. The driver was sitting at the wheel behind his plastic screen with a huge grin on his face. 'Fire station or Hospital, madam? Or perhaps the TV studio?'

'One and a child to the fire station please,' said a mother who was fit to explode. 'And don't even think about saying …'

'Exterminate! … exterminate! …'

'That's it, Frank! Next time, there will be no dinner for you, it'll be straight off to bed, do you hear?'

'Yes, Mum,' replied a contrite little boy.

'Four pounds-thirty please, no charge for the saucepan.'

Thirty minutes later, after struggling through the usual traffic, the door of the bus swung open for the Dalek to step out onto the pavement. 'Best of luck,' said the grinning driver. 'Though you would have got here sooner if you had used your Tardis.'

Fortunately, the bus stop was right outside the fire station, so Mrs Bennet was relieved of further embarrassment. 'Right, here we are, Frank. It'll soon be off now. Don't ever ask me to play Doctor Who games with you again, or Batman, or Spiderman. From now on, it's Ludo or Snakes and Ladders.'

'Good afternoon, Madam,' said the smartly turned-out sub-officer with a sympathetic smile. 'Another Dalek, I see? Saucepans are not a good idea. Putting them on is always easier than getting them off, as you have found out. Come on through and we'll see what we can do, shall we?' The kind fireman led mother and son into a workshop which was equipped with an array of complicated looking equipment. 'What's your name, sonny?'

'Frank,' said the boy as he nervously looked around the room.

'Okay, Frank, come and sit over here, this shouldn't take too long. The boy followed the fireman to a chair by a large window and sat down as instructed.

'Ok,' said the fireman. 'If you are good, we might allow you to climb up into the fire engine cab for a look around. You would like that, wouldn't you?'

'Yes please,' said Frank who was no longer looking so nervous.

Turning back to the boy's mother, he said, 'Now then, Mrs Bennet, let's see if we can get that saucepan off of your head, shall we?'

The End

The Last Time

You will never be the same
From the moment you hold your
baby in your arms.
You may long for the person you were before;
When you had freedom and time,
And nothing particularly to worry about.

You will know tiredness like you never knew it before.
Days will run into yet more days that are exactly the same as the one before;
Full of feeding and burping, nappy changes and crying,
Whining and fighting,
Naps or lack of naps,
It might seem like a never-ending cycle.

But don't forget;

There is a last time for everything.

There will come a time when you will breast feed your baby for the last time.

When they will fall asleep on you after a long day's struggle;

And it will be the last time you ever hold your sleeping child in that way.

One day you will carry them on your hip, not realising this will be the last time you will ever do that.

You will scrub their hair in the bath one night

And from that night on they will want to bathe alone.

They will hold your hand to cross the road, then never reach for it again.

They will creep into your room at midnight for cuddles,

And it will be the last time you ever awaken to this.

One afternoon you will sing "The wheels on the bus" and do all the actions;

Then never sing them that song again.

They will kiss you goodbye at the school gate,

Then on the next day they will ask to walk to the gate alone.

You will read a final bedtime story and wipe your last dirty face.

They will run to you with arms raised for the very last time.

The thing is, you will not even know it is the last time,

Until there are no more times.

And even then, it will take you a while to realize.

So, while you are living in these times;

Remember there are only so many of them.

And when they are gone, you will yearn for just one more day of those special moments.

For one last time.

Alone

There has been no let-up in the rain since the middle of this cold autumn day. Street lights are now reflected in the deep puddles which dominate the cracked pavers. Water flows freely in the gully alongside the quiet road. Drains are no longer able to allow the water to enter the hidden network of pipes below the surface of the avenue. Water cascades down from many of the gutters belonging to the buildings along the row of smart terraced dwellings. Occasionally a passing vehicle sweeps through a large puddle in the road, causing water to splash freely over the pavement.

A tall man is standing in the shadow of one of the many trees which line the avenue. He steps back as yet another cascade of splashed water sweeps across the pavement, just missing his legs. It is, however, of no consequence, as the man's lower legs and feet are already soaked, not being protected beneath the beige gabardine mac he is wearing. He doesn't notice. The collar of that mac is turned up beneath the trilby hat which, every so often, allows water to drip down his collar from the brim as he looks up to the first-floor window on the other side of the avenue.

The man reaches into his coat pocket, from which he extracts a twenty pack of cigarettes. Leaning forward over the pack in an attempt to keep it dry he extracts the last cigarette, which he places between his lips before carelessly tossing the empty pack onto the water-covered pavement beyond the meagre protection of the tree. The man is now fumbling in his other pocket, feeling for a Swan Vestas matchbox from which he carefully lifts a match. On the third attempt, the match splutters into sparks to be immediately followed by a small but intense flame. For a brief moment, the man's gaunt face is illuminated when he draws on the cigarette to create a soft glow as he inhales the smoke into his lungs.

With smoke coming from his nostrils, the man again lifts his eyes to peer through the slanting rain at the illuminated window opposite. The curtains have not been drawn. His eyes take in the shaded ceiling light, the only thing he can see from below. He is waiting to see if any of them come to the window. He has waited in the rain for at least an hour now. He inhales more smoke, holding the cigarette in the cup of his hand in an attempt to keep it dry. He removes a shred of tobacco from between his lips. Suddenly, he sees a change of light in the window that is occupying his attention, presumably someone is crossing the room. He is fully alert, unaware of the rain pattering on his upturned face. He involuntarily takes a half step forward. The curtain is disturbed by the movement of someone coming to the window. His heart skips a beat, a few more seconds, then …*Splashshsh!* He jumps back, but too late. The rear car lights are already dissolving into the rain which shows no sign of easing off. The man quickly looks up at the window. The curtains have been drawn across.

With cold water dripping from his soaked mac the man curses as he focuses once again on the window. There is a narrow chink of light in the centre of the carelessly drawn curtains. A silhouette flits across the space that has been the focus of the man's attention as he stands there in the darkness. One of the children. Timothy or Julie? He is not sure which one it was. How he is missing those children. It has been seven weeks now. Seven long miserable weeks since he has seen his children and seven weeks since he has held a bottle to his lips. He had known for several months that Linda was playing away. The signs were all there. Perfume she had never used before, new underwear, telephone calls that went silent when he picked up. He could not blame her. He had been on the bottle since his best mate had been killed in Aden back in sixty-five. *Dishonourable discharge,* they called it, after the man had served his stretch in the military prison. That Lieutenant deserved more than the kicking our man had given him when they returned from that fated patrol. That cowardly officer had just left Chas, alone in the dust and filth. The man had tried so hard to put his life back together when he eventually got home. He had watched their twin babies grow, with a mixture of pride and resentment. They had occupied so much of Linda's time. He had needed her so much, as never before. The girl he had left when they sailed away on the troop ship, was gone. Her love had gone cold. He had tried to explain his feelings, but how could he, when he didn't understand them himself?

Friends, who had drunk to his health and safe return from South Arabia the week before departure, had turned their backs on him. Employment had been difficult to find. A series of Security Guard jobs was the best he had managed. Whisky had become his only friend. If only Linda had tried to understand, get him to offload, find him some help.

It was the evening when she said that she was going round to a girl friend called Diane, that changed everything. He had had a few on his way home, but was sober enough to agree to stay home with the children who were busy with their homework. As she had come out from the bedroom, he had noticed the perfume. Why did she need to put that on if she were just going round to Diane's? On impulse, having checked that the twins were still busy, he slipped out to follow his wife … to this smart house close to the park. He had watched as she rang the door-bell, as the man answered the door, as he took her in his arms, as the door closed behind them. He had returned home that evening to find the twins, having finished their homework, watching television. He allowed them a further half hour then supervised them as they prepared for bed. Linda didn't return until gone eleven-o-clock. By then, he had reached the bottom of his bottle. He didn't mean to hit her. He had intended to talk, to plead, to … He was in shock. He had never done that before. Without a word, she had pushed herself up from the floor and left the room. He could hear frightened voices upstairs. He sat, dazed, on the sofa. His head was spinning. He felt sick. He sat back on the sofa as the room spun around him. He was vaguely aware of the sound of the front door opening and closing … of hurried footsteps on the path outside … of silence.

Seven weeks of silence from his family. Seven weeks without the false comfort of alcohol. Seven weeks of soul searching. Forty-two days of self-loathing. Forty-two days of loneliness. Throughout that time, he had known where to look. Should he just knock on that door and demand the return of his family? Could he? What could he say that would ever forgive him for that punch? Perhaps they were safer where they were. Safer from him?

The man drops the cigarette end onto the sodden pavement and, without thinking, places his wet shoe on it with a turn of the foot. He continues watching the chink of light. What is he waiting for? What is he hoping for? There is no hope for him. He has forfeited his right to be a husband and father. They deserve better. He hopes that the man behind those curtains will give them the love and security he is no longer capable of.

With a final glance at the window, the man lifts his rain-coat collar further up his wet neck, turns and walks slowly away, in the direction of Canal Street. On the wet pavement, where he had stood for so long, there is a soggy cigarette box on which the word *STRAND* can clearly be seen.

The End

Fayella

Neville had always been a bit of a loner, preferring to keep his own company. He didn't make friends easily and small talk was something he preferred to avoid as much as possible. His parents despaired of ever welcoming a future daughter-in-law into the family, and as for grandchildren …. Young men of his age were into soccer, cricket, formula 1, pop music and girls. Not so, Neville. His one passion, apart from trading in company shares, was collecting amusement parks and funfairs. Well not so much collecting as visiting. He had travelled the length of Britain in the pursuit of his hobby, and the continent of Europe was on the agenda when time allowed. The USA was to be his swansong at some point in the future.

Some might say that Neville was a bit strange. Why would anyone want to go to leisure parks alone? Surely, they were something to enjoy in a group along with other friends, weren't they? Not so with Neville. In his view, this was not for sharing, as to do so would be an unwelcome distraction. Apart from other novelties, he enjoyed the various rides. Not for him the silly lifting of arms in the air at exhilarating moments. Such foolishness was simply an attempt to display coolness. But it was not cool to draw attention to one's self in his view. Oh no, he would simply sit still and absorb the ride, although he would have preferred it if he were the sole occupant of the pod/train/boat/log, or whatever.

At the time of our story Neville had taken himself off to a theme park in East Kent where semi-educational rides were advertised. He had only recently found out about this place on an obscure website and was not sure what to expect. It was the word "rides" that attracted him, particularly as the park was fairly close to his home which was set in substantial grounds. This park must be worth a visit, he surmised.

His first impression upon arrival in his open-top MG was one of surprise, and intrigue. For starters, there were very few people about, although it was approaching eleven-o-clock. Also, it was quiet, just soft ethereal music, the sort that is played in the meditation sessions he was sometimes engaged in when he had had to endure an uncomfortable conversation with strangers and dealers. Having paid the required entry fee, as per his usual habit Neville wandered around the various attractions for a while to see what was on offer and to make mental notes on “must do’s” and “maybe’s.” He then headed for the refreshment area where he purchased a can of Cola which he consumed while gazing around this strange place. As far as he had been able to work out there were three “must do’s”; one was a simulated space station docking experience, another was a simulated drive of a wagon with a team of six horses passing through a busy town. The third, and possibly the least exciting of the three, was a pod-ride through a seventeenth century community living a nomadic life of self-sufficiency, which included various crafts and farming methods.

As he sat there drinking his Cola, Neville was aware of a strange atmosphere about the park. Nothing he could put his finger on. Just a feeling. The few customers he observed all looked happy and normal for such a place, the staff were friendly and welcoming. So, what was it then that was bothering him? Perhaps the unusual music for such a place? Yes, that must be it. Deciding that he was being fanciful Neville dropped his empty can into a nearby bin and opted for the least interesting ride first before building up to the more interesting ones. So, it was to the seventeenth century pod ride he headed to start the day. He was rather pleased to see that there was no queue as he stepped up to the platform. With no member of staff in attendance Neville waited for the first slowly approaching pod which emerged from a concealed exit. There were no people in it so he could quickly seat himself on the comfortable seat and place the bar over his lap. Just before swinging around the corner which would draw the pod into the concealed interior Neville took a last glance across the park. Was it his imagination that all the people in the vicinity of the attraction were standing still, and seeming to be staring at him?

As daylight changed to a reddish glow which suggested an evening setting, Neville's senses were invaded by the smell of newly cut hay, of smoke and the suggestion of something unpleasant, raw sewage perhaps? The pod was slipping quietly between dwellings which were a mixture of mud and rough timbers with long grass spread across the tops. Every so often the pod swung around in order to allow the occupant to peer through crude windows and doors into the dark interiors lit only by candles and the flickering light from fires which burned on hard-packed mud floors. As his eyes became accustomed to the gloom, Neville could make out the shadowy shapes of the occupants, adults in various postures holding tools and pots, children sitting on low benches or playing on floors. As he passed each door, Neville had a strange feeling of being an intruder into a world in which he didn't belong. He was aware of the prickling of hairs at the back of his neck.

The pod swung around yet again as Neville took in the horrific tableau of a man cutting the throat of a tethered goat. He gave a violent shudder as his nostrils were overcome with the iron smell of blood. Was it purely imagination that the eyes of the man seemed to follow the slowly moving pod with its startled passenger? He knew that none of this was real, and yet …

With a sense of relief Neville allowed himself to sit back as the pod turned a sharp corner. Surely things would become more relaxing as village became open countryside. In the distance a hay rick was being built by two men wielding pitchforks. A blackbird was singing its throaty song. The pod travelled past various farm implements which were resting in long grass. This was better, Neville's heart settled to a normal rhythm, until suddenly the pod swung away from the open space before entering a forest of overgrown bushes and plants amidst a variety of trees, mainly oak. The scenery became darker. Neville could barely make out the shapes of animals or possibly people, hidden in the gloom. He was aware of movement and of rustling in the deeper shadows. The pod continued its slow journey through the tangle of trees, every so often swinging around to present its passenger with a different perspective of the same scenery, if scenery it could be called, for there was little to be made out in the darkness. All of Neville's senses were at a high pitch; smell; hearing; sight; touch. He was expecting something, but what?

When that something did happen, it came as a shock …

The girl peered through the undergrowth. She knew exactly where she was and what she intended if and when the "thing" made an appearance. It had been a while since the last one had appeared. She had no way of measuring time, for nothing ever changed in the gloom of her surroundings. She knew every tree, plant and rock, every animal whether large or small. She knew the boundaries beyond which she should never wander. This was her home, but for how much longer?

She had no idea of her age; it was sufficient to compare herself with the few others that lived here. Some were old with grey hair and wrinkles over their bodies, others were smaller than her, shapeless. When unclothed she had been aware of the changing shape of her own body. How her hips were now wider than her middle and how her chest had developed in the same way as the grown women. Her hair had grown long and was now below her slim waist. Apart from dim reflections in water she had never seen her own face.

She had no concept of day or night, for in this place the light never changed. Something told her however, that this would be the moment she had been waiting for. She was determined to find a future away from the darkness of this forest, and the fate that awaited her. The man who had been selected to lay with her was cruel and loathsome. She shuddered at the thought of allowing him to come near her, let alone touch her. Whatever awaited her in the forbidden world would surely be better than the act of making a baby with that man, as was considered her duty according to the elders.

With that thought came the fear of the unknown course she was determined to follow. She could see the path upon which the

"thing" would pass. She had waited here for many sleeps and something inside her said that the wait was over, she would be ready. As had become her custom she crouched down behind a bush and waited. Regardless of the warmth that surrounded her she was consumed with the shivers. She was afraid. Where would the "thing" take her? she wondered. Some said that it would go to the very edge of the world where it would tip anyone foolish enough to mount it into the black pit. Others said that it would come alive and eat anyone on it. The girl was on the verge of turning back to the village to face her fate when she heard the familiar sound approaching. Already on her feet, she stepped out from behind the bush and waited in the darkness as the sound drew nearer.

Neville peered into the gloom, filled with curiosity as to what the next tableau would reveal. He was not expecting the sudden shock of a body striking him with a painful blow to his head, nor to be engulfed in limbs thrashing about above him as he was pressed into the seat. It was the scream that sent shockwaves through his senses, or was it two different screams? His and … who else? With his face smothered in strands of hair and his legs trapped beneath the seat he at least had one free hand with which to try to push the weight from his body. The screams continued as his hand encountered something soft. Panicking, he pushed with all his strength in an attempt to release himself from whatever had pounced upon him. He yelped as something bit the soft flesh of his hand, in defence and retaliation he swung his free arm and clouted the animal on its hairy head. The high-pitched scream changed to a single word *'Ouch!'* It was clearly the voice of a female.

'What the …?' With renewed effort Neville placed his arm around the body of this wild person and attempted to pull her away from his trapped legs.

'*Get your filthy hands off my chest!*'

Quickly repositioning his hand Neville shouted, *'Get off my lap you stupid bitch. You're over-playing the part. I should report you to the park manager!'*

'And I should report you to the elders for an unchosen man molesting me. They'll hang you from the village oak for that!' Whilst saying this, the girl untangled herself from Neville's limbs and sank down onto the seat beside him. 'Why are you on the "thing" anyway. You know it's punishable by lashing.'

'Oh, is it? Then why have you just jumped on, and anyway, lashing is against the law.'

'Don't know about that, I just know they do it. Aren't you afraid of where the "thing" is taking us?' By this time the pod had turned a corner and they could see light ahead.

'Ha! Why should I be afraid? Unless there are more of you waiting to attack me? This ride should come with a warning.'

'We're always being warned not to come near the "thing", you must know that. Who are you and why are you on it?'

'My name is Neville and I'm in the pod because I paid for it and I thought it would be educational. I didn't realise it included being attacked by a member of staff. Are all the other rides like this?'

'You speak of things I do not understand. I'm sorry if I hurt you. I didn't know you were on this "thing". Are you trying to escape as well?'

'I assume you are a student doing a summer job to help with the fees, but I'm sure you're not supposed to throw yourself at the customers. What's your name?'

'I don't understand what you are saying. My name is Fayella and I'm getting away from here because I will not allow that man near me. He stinks!'

'What man? Has someone been bothering you? You must report him to the management, Fay …Fay …'

'Ella … Fayella. Look! The darkness is leaving us. I can see things like never before, it's …it's … exciting and scary, it's making my eyes water.'

'Ella,' said Neville after a pause. 'How long have you been in here?'

'I have been in the village since I was born of course. This is the furthest I have ever been in my life.' Fayella continued looking around with half closed streaming eyes.

'You mean … you live here?'

'Yes, but no more. I don't know where the "thing" is taking me but I think I can jump off if I don't like where it's going.'

For a moment Neville was lost for words. 'Tell me this is a big joke. I don't believe any of this.' As he spoke, the pod turned another corner before emerging into sunlight. The girl beside him let out a gasp and covered her eyes. 'I can't see! My eyes are hurting! What's happening to me?'

Neville was taken by surprise by the obvious distress the girl was in. Without conscious thought, he pulled her into his body and cradled her head into his chest in an attempt to comfort her and to protect her eyes. For the first time he was able to see this strange person who had attacked him. Her dress appeared to be made from a mixture of fur and leather. She was wearing laced up moccasin type shoes. Her black hair was long and tangled, clearly in need of a wash. Her body odour was strong. She was clutching his arm as she pressed her face into his sweater. The pod was moving slowly toward a yard where several others were scattered amongst work benches. An overall clad figure approached as the pod came to an abrupt standstill.

'What the hell are you two doing in there?' he demanded. 'This pod was scheduled to veer off the main track to come into the maintenance yard. You should not have been in it. Go on, hop it. Go and find somewhere private to do your canoodling. You youngsters have no shame. No knowing what you get up to in the dark. What's up with her anyhow? Come on girl, out of there. I've got work to do on this pod.'

Pushing the bar forward Neville said, 'Come on Ella, we have to get out of here. Cover your eyes, I'll hold on to you. You're quite safe, trust me.' Carefully, Neville led the girl out of the yard and made directly for the park exit and the car park. Fayella held her hands over her eyes throughout the walk so didn't see the strange looks they were given from people as they passed by. With relief Neville guided Fayella to his car and was glad that he had thought to close the soft top after parking it. Having opened the passenger door and lowered the girl onto the seat, he skipped round the front to let himself in on the other side.

'Okay Ella. We are in my car. Are your eyes still hurting?'

'They feel sore and I'm frightened to open them in case I'm blind, like old Sheena, where are we?'

'As I said, we are in my car, in the car park.'

'I don't understand. Are we in danger in this Ka?'

'No, we are perfectly safe. Try opening your eyes a little and slowly spread your fingers so you can look through them.'

'Oh, I can see light! So much light, where is it coming from?'

'From the sun.'

'What is this "Sun"?

'You are serious, aren't you? I can't begin to understand any of this. Ella, please tell me honestly, have you always lived in that dark place amongst those trees?'

'Of course! Where else is there?'

'Where are your parents, your family?'

'I don't know what they are.'

'Who has been looking after you?'

'The elders see to our needs and tell us what to do. They also punish us if we are bad.'

'My god. I must be dreaming all of this, surely.'

'I have dreams, but I don't understand them, are we in the same dream now, Nev-Hill?'

'Neville. My name is Neville. We can't stay here. Where would you like me to take you?'

'I don't know. Anywhere that stinky man won't find me. I don't want to have his baby.'

'Ella, can you see anything other than light? Try moving your fingers a little more apart and look at me.'

Slowly, the girl opened her fingers wider as she turned to face Neville. 'The light is so bright, like too many flaming torches, and it's hurting my eyes, but not so much now. I think I can see you, but you're just a dark shadow. How can you be just a shadow?'

‘Ella, cover your eyes with one hand for a moment and give me your other hand. Trust me.’

She was starting to feel that she could trust this man who had such a kind soft voice and a sweet smell, not like the elders. What choice did she have? She was still alive, and she had not, so far, been punished. She did as Neville had told her. She felt her free hand being taken into the man’s hand. It was soft and warm. He lifted her hand to his face where she felt his ears, his cheeks, chin and nose. To her surprise, there was no hair on his face.

‘There, now you can tell that I’m not just a shadow. I think your eyes will become used to the light, just give them time. Shut them tight now, and move your hand away. Go on. That’s it. My god, Ella has anyone ever told you that you are beautiful?’

‘What is “Beautiful”? I do not understand that word. Is it bad?’

‘You are. It means … a pleasure to look at.’

‘Are you “beautiful” Nev-Hill?’

‘Yes, I suppose I am, I’ve never really thought about it. I’m going to drive you to my home, it’ll take about forty minutes. Try opening your eyes a little as we go.’

'I don't understand this "drive" and "forty mints" is it something I must pay? I have nothing except the clothes I wear. I can work for you, clean your hut, sweep the earth on your floor, catch and cook rats, repair your roof.'

'Nothing to pay. Now you mustn't be frightened. We will be moving fast in this car and you will hear traffic. Nothing will hurt you. Do you trust me?'

'Yes Nev-Hill, I think I trust you. And I won't let this "traffic" thing worry me if you say it's safe.'

'Okay, I'm just going to strap you in so that you are even more safe, then I will strap myself in. You may find that you begin to enjoy the ride.'

There was nothing in Fayella's life that could have prepared her for the experience of that journey. The comfort of a soft seat; the movement; the noise; the smell of leather, of freshly cut grass; of the man's aftershave. Uppermost in the turmoil of her senses was the ever-changing shades of light. At first, it was too bright to make any lasting impression but, gradually she started discerning flashing shades of green. The shadow beside her transformed into the vague shape of a man. The invasive yellow of his sweater slowly gave way to the shape of his head with the golden brown of his hair. It was all too much to take in, so most of the journey was seen through half closed eyes. He had said that he would take her to his home. What were his intentions? Was he going to return her to the elders? Would he want to keep her to make babies? Or did he just want her to keep his hut clean? He had a gentle way of touching her and talking to her. He had not shown any anger. She had to trust him. Before the journey ended, Fayella managed to open her eyes wider and focus more in the confines of the car. Apart from the seats it was all hard edged, unlike anything she had seen before. She tried to keep her eyes away from the front and side walls which had constantly moving images. Throughout the time they sat together in the box the man kept telling her about the things he said they were passing, although she had no idea what he was talking about, apart from the fact she didn't want to look at the walls of the box thing. She guessed they were moving to somewhere, and very quickly, so long as it took her further away from the stinky man and the elders she didn't care.

With a sense of relief Neville turned the car off the main road, through a wooden gate and onto the gravel drive leading up to his large Edwardian house. As he did so, he wondered what Ella would make of the size of both house and grounds. He glanced at her as he drove up to the front steps and said, 'This is it, Ella. My home. Stay there and I'll come round and let you out.'

As she stepped out onto the gravel with her eyes once again closed Neville took her hand and led her to the bottom of the wide time-aged steps. 'You have to step up here, Ella. Can you open your eyes to see the steps in front of us?'

She paused for a moment and started blinking as her eyes opened. 'I can see them!' she cried in amazement. 'I can see them clearly. I can see a high wall with lots of holes.'

'That's my house, it's windows you can see.'

'What are these windows?'

'I'll explain when we're inside. Turn around and tell me what you see.'

Fayella did as asked and gasped as she clutched onto Neville. She was shaking violently. 'What's wrong, Ella? What did you see?'

'It's too big and far away. I can see trees but they are so far. And there's something big above us but there isn't anything holding it up. It could all fall down on us. I can already see stuff moving up there.'

'Puzzled, Neville followed the girl's gaze then started laughing. 'That's the sky. Haven't you ever seen the sky before?'

'Please don't laugh at me Nev-Hill, I'm so scared. Everything is so different and confusing. You have to help me … please?'

'I'm sorry, Ella. This situation is strange to me as well, I think we will need to help each other.' It was at this point that Neville came to realise the enormity of the whole situation. How would Fayella ever be able to absorb all the new sites and experiences? Every aspect of modern life that is accepted as normal would be new and complex for her, from using a toilet to watching a TV, from safely crossing a road to shopping in a supermarket. Assuming she remained with him he could see that he had a difficult task ahead. Would she remain with him? Where else could she go? Without doubt, she was an extremely beautiful girl and the idea of taking her into his home was becoming an attractive and exciting prospect.

Then there was the question of where she had come from. Was there really another hidden dimension which remains hidden and separate? He had heard of the possibility of a parallel universe and wormholes, but surely that was nonsense? He had never given the idea any credence. If the girl had somehow crossed an invisible barrier what would happen to her now? Would her body be able to cope with colds and viruses? Then there were the legal implications. No birth certificate, no passport, no medical records. She would be regarded as an illegal immigrant if discovered.

With these thoughts filling his head Neville took Fayella's arm and led her up the steps to the front door. He could feel her body tensing as he unlocked the door and pushed it open. He attempted to imagine seeing the interior through her eyes. Everyday items and furniture that he would normally not notice would be totally beyond her experience and knowledge.

'Nev-Hill. I don't understand. Where are we? What is this place? I thought you were taking me to your hut. It's all so big and frightening. Can we go to your hut now?'

'This is my "hut" as you call it, Ella. It's where I live. It's my house.'

'But it's so big! There must be many of your people living here.'

'No … Just me.' Spontaneously, Neville added, 'And you, Ella. This can also be your home if you want to stay here with me.'

'So that we can make babies together? I think I would like that. Do you have to ask the elders first?'

'No, Ella, there are no elders. We can talk about that another time.'

This conversation was taking place just inside the still open front door and was going somewhere Neville was uncomfortable with. The idea of making babies with this beautiful and innocent girl was making him blush, even causing a slight stir in the front of his trousers. He cleared his throat before continuing. 'We don't need to think about babies, let's just concentrate on getting you sorted out. As you have already experienced, you have got a lot to learn if you are to remain away from the place you came from. I would like to help you. We can learn together.'

'Yes, then can we make babies?'

With a sigh Neville replied, 'Come on, I'll show you around.'

'First, I need the hole. Where is it?'

'The hole? What hole?'

'I need to do a splash, and maybe a plop. Where is it?'

That is how the education of Fayella started. It was fortunate indeed that she was a fast learner. She loved the guest bedroom which she insisted upon referring to as her "hut", although it was several nights before Neville was able to persuade her to sleep on the bed rather than under it. She also loved the clothes and shoes Neville bought for her from his computer. She had no desire to leave the house and grounds for the first three months. She loved listening to Neville as he patiently explained every new thing she saw and used. He in turn, was enjoying looking at his life and home afresh, as though through her eyes. She loved the stories he read to her from his books, particularly as she got into the habit of nestling against Neville so that she could follow the words on the page. When he spent time on his computer, working on his share portfolio, she was content to wander around the grounds and even managed to start a small vegetable garden, using seeds Neville had bought on-line. During that time, other seeds were growing; the seeds of love. Neville was very much aware of his growing love for this girl who had literally dropped into his life. Fayella still didn't fully understand the concept of love. She only knew that she wanted him to be her man, and she, his woman giving him lots of babies, and that she wanted nothing more than to be in his company as much as possible, and to please him. While, for those first three months, she had happily taken on the tasks of cleaning and cooking basic meals for her man she was determined that they should soon make a baby together, although she had only a vague understanding of how that could be achieved. She understood that it would be necessary for them to sleep together in the same hut but beyond that, she had no idea.

A day came after that first three months when Fayella felt ready to go out beyond the grounds to learn more about this new life she had entered. Neville welcomed the idea as he had begun to feel like a prisoner in his own home, not having been able to leave her on her own. Perhaps a day out would ease the tension he was under in respect of his growing feelings toward his Ella. He so much wanted to take her in his arms to kiss her and to hold her.

So, what was holding him back? She had been showing signs that she might feel the same way, but where would it lead to? He still had no idea from where she came. How was any of this possible? Would she simply disappear in the same way that she had arrived in his life? Was he prepared to risk heartbreak? What could he tell his parents who so much wanted a grandchild?

Without a conscious decision, Neville found himself driving in the direction of the theme park where this had all started. He didn't tell Fayella however, for he didn't know how she would react to the thought of being taken back there. Maybe he would get some answers to his many questions? Having already been prepared for what the outside world would look like by means of Neville's television, Fayella found that she enjoyed the thrill of the drive. She loved the feel of the sun on her face and wind in her hair. The open views of distant hills, trees and church spires quickly brought a radiant smile to her face. 'Oh Nev-Hill, this is so beautiful!' she shouted into the slipstream.

'Not nearly as beautiful as you, Ella. I'm so glad you're enjoying being away from the house.' As he spoke, Neville patted her knee affectionately. Having replaced his hand on the steering wheel he was surprised and pleased when Fayella eased his hand back from the wheel and replaced it on her bare knee. Glancing quickly at her, he noticed the quiet smile on her face and continued resting his hand on her knee until the demands of driving safely required both hands on the wheel once again.

In no time it seemed to them both, Neville swung the car into the narrow lane which led to the theme park. However, he was startled when he turned into the entrance to find that he had driven into a large field which was covered in hop poles, all of which were holding a near-ready harvest.

'Why have we come here?' asked Fayella who was taking in the scene. 'I don't like it here, can we go?'

'This was … I don't understand. I know this is the right place, I remember that barn we passed back there.'

'Can I help you?' enquired a lady dressed in overalls who was approaching the car. 'Harvest is not till the middle of September if that's what you've come for,' she said.

'No. I'm looking for the theme park which is near here. We must have come the wrong way. Do you know where it is by any chance?'

With a chuckle the lady replied, 'Ain't no theme parks around these parts, sorry I can't help you.'

'For how long has this hop farm been here?'

'Don't rightly know. Been in my husband's family for generations. Anyhow, must get on, hope you find what you're looking for.'

As the lady disappeared between two lines of tall poles Neville sat and stared at the crop for a while before turning to Fayella, taking both of her hands in his and saying, 'Ella, I don't really know where you have come from, you're a total mystery to me, but I've fallen in love with you. Even if I could return you to your people I wouldn't know how, and I certainly wouldn't want to. Do you think you could be happy living with me for the rest of your life? Because that's what I would like.'

'Oh, yes please, Nev-Hill. I don't ever want to be anywhere else with anyone else. I like you teaching me. You are so kind and gentle with me. If I'm going to live with you for ever, can I move into your hut so that we can sleep together and make babies?'

'If that's what you really want. We have no further business here. Let's go and never come back. You can certainly move into my hut tonight and all the nights to come. Now, we aren't too far away from where my parents live. I think it is time they met you, although heaven knows what they'll make of you.'

The End

Vibrationis Abductor Pollicis

For a moment the three people stood shoulder to shoulder as they examined the Xray which the tallest of them was holding before the light screen.

'What we see here is very much as I feared, Mister and Misses Lincoln. Your daughter's condition has become severe, so-much-so that urgent treatment cannot be put off any longer. I have seen this condition before, but never as advanced as this. Observe the tendons and muscles, the deformity of the bones in the digits which, apart from the thumb and index finger, have become fixed in that un-natural state. As for the thumb and index finger, they are now subject to uncontrollable spasms of rapid movement at a speed similar to the wings of a humming bird. One might be forgiven for confusing this condition with that known as "Median Nerve Palsy" but this is different. It's incredible. With your permission I intend writing a paper on this new phenomenon which I am beginning to see more of, particularly in the young.'

'What's to be done, doctor?' piped in Mrs Lincoln as she gazed at the disturbing image in front of her eyes. 'Is there some sort of treatment? An operation, drugs, or something? Anything?'

'There must be something you can do, doctor,' added her husband. 'It has got to the point where the child is unable to look up, or speak to us. She has her eyes fixed on that closed fist from morning till night. It's taken over her body and mind. She eats whatever is put in front of her without looking at it or seeming to taste it, she no longer hears us when we speak to her, it's as though the thing that's taken over her hand is invading her brain. You have to do something.'

Massaging his chin, the doctor stared at the image for a moment before switching off the light screen and turning to the distraught parents, both of whom were staring at him in a combination of hope, fear, and expectancy. 'Drugs may become a long-term remedy further down the road to recovery, but I fear that an operation will be unavoidable in the short term. I say "fear" with reason, you see there are risks involved. Apart from possible damage to the hand, there is the risk of confusion leading to loss of direction and severe depression. You will have to be with her constantly as she emerges from a bad place and starts on her path of rehab in which she will once again be able to enjoy a new life of discovery. It will not be easy for her, or you.'

Taking in the enormity of what Doctor Finch had just told them the child's distraught parents turned to face the chair on which she was sitting, oblivious of the three other people in the room with her. With hunched shoulders Debbie continued staring at her right hand, the subject of the strained conversation. Her thumb and index finger were a blur, so rapid was the movement in both digits.

'Darling, are you listening to what the doctor is saying about your condition?' enquired Mrs Lincoln as she stepped across the room to put her arm around the rocking shoulder of her daughter. There was no reaction, so her mother stooped lower to repeat the question. 'Debbie, sweetheart, do you understand that the doctor must operate on your hand? It's for the best.' The girl gave no indication of either hearing or understanding as the three adults watched the thumb which continued to vibrate. With tears rolling down her cheeks Mrs Lincoln straightened and looked at her husband before turning to the doctor and quietly saying, 'We agree to the operation, how soon can it be done?'

'I can do it right now. It won't take more than five minutes; I'll fetch my instruments while you get Debbie onto the couch, if you would be so kind.'

With Debbie securely held on the couch by her parents, Doctor Finch bent over the girl and gently lifted the effected hand as he concentrated on where best to make his entry. As he did so, the never still thumb and index finger continued their movement as the girl's eyes remained fixed.

'Ah yes, I have it,' muttered the doctor with satisfaction. 'I'm going in, now. Be prepared for the shock and reaction, no knowing how she'll come out of it.' With that warning, Dr Finch turned his back to the parents and did his work with much care and concentration. Mrs Lincoln was unable to look at the doctor's hunched back as he worked, so she focused her attention on the calendar hanging on the wall near the door. October the third, perhaps a date she would always remember however this turned out. Suddenly the relative quietness of the room was pierced by an ear-splitting scream followed by the clatter of an object falling into a kidney bowl.

'It's okay Honey,' soothed Mr Lincoln, 'We're here with you.'

'Dad? Is that you? Where am I? Who is that man in the white coat?' Where's my mobile?'

'It's okay, Sweetheart,' said Mrs Lincoln. 'This is Doctor Finch; he's brought you back to us.'

'Mummy! It's you! Oh, my goodness, where have I been?'

'We don't know, Honey, but wherever it was, you're back with us now. This is the first time we've heard your voice for nearly a year. It's so good to have you back and to be able to see your pretty eyes again.'

Taking her eyes from her mother's smiling face and looking down at her outstretched right hand, Debbie repeated her question, 'Where is my mobile?'

'I can answer that, my dear.' said the doctor. 'I managed to prise your hand open sufficient to get the battery out. The screen went dead, you screamed, and the phone is sitting in that kidney bowl.'

'But I need … I want … how can … Oh my, I feel so free! Look at the window, the sky, the trees, the birds. I had forgotten.'

'I know, Honey,' said Mr Lincoln as he hugged his daughter, it was the first time he had been able to do that for a long time. 'Let's go and find you some real friends.'

The End

Wheels

Traffic heading for the coast on this warm sunny morning in August is fairly heavy, not that this is of any concern to the three young men who are steering their motor-cycles around the slowly moving cars. They are not concerned which lane they have to use so long as they can stay on the move as they head for their intended destination. They are all wearing black protective leathers which are adorned with various images and words which are beyond the understanding of the average motorist they are effortlessly speeding passed. Beneath their highly decorated helmets all three have black shaggy hair and beards. On the face of it, these are not young men to whom one would feel an instant warmth, and it would be fair to say that the coastal village, to which they are heading, whilst welcoming day trippers, would most likely not be sorry if they rode on passed. But they do not do that. The car park at the top of the village, which is as far as the road goes, is suddenly consumed by the roar of the three motor-cycles. Holiday makers and day trippers scatter as the riders obliviously pass through them while heading for the area within the car park, which is designated for motor cycles only.

After much seemingly unnecessary revving-up each of the three motor cycle engines give way to silence. Conversation in the immediate vicinity once again becomes possible as the three riders lift their respective helmets whilst still sitting astride their silent, machines. One or two men are seen to break away from their families as they saunter across the tarmac to admire the bikes. They are ignored by the three riders who secretly enjoy the attention their highly polished machines are receiving from the men who respectfully, or nervously, maintain a short distance between themselves and the black cladded young men who are chatting and laughing together.

'Right,' says the shortest of the three, 'let's go and find a pub. My throat feels like one-hundred grade sandpaper. Having secured their bikes, the men saunter in the general direction of the main village street which leads to the quay. It is noticeable to any observer that whilst folk need to constantly dodge around each other as they walk down the narrow street, a cleared pathway constantly appears, as if by magic, in front of the three leather booted young men. At the first public house they come across, the lads stoop through the low doorway into a dimly lit public bar.

‘Three pints of your best local ale,’ calls the tallest of the three without waiting to attract the attention of the woman behind the bar. The lads have no difficulty finding a vacant table in the bar, as other customers clearly prefer to be in the garden at the rear of the building on this sunny day. With foaming beer in front of them, the men take several gulps from their glasses before unfastening and removing their leather jackets. Each is wearing a white T-shirt with the same picture of a flaming motor cycle flying through a star-studded space. The bar tender surreptitiously watches them between serving other customers who constantly appear from the garden doorway to replenish their glasses.

Three empty glasses stand on the table as the men don their jackets without fastening them and head for the door. The bar tender lets out a breath and relaxes as the doorway once again lets in the sunlight that had momentarily been blocked as the friends playfully jostle each other while ducking under the lintel. Together, they saunter down the crowded street. It is their intention to make for the quay for no other reason than to soak up the holiday atmosphere and enjoy the scenery of this popular resort which could of course include admiring any young ladies who might attract their attention. The delight of a Cornish pasty is also on the agenda.

This has been the first opportunity in quite a while that the three friends have been able to spend such a day together. Hospitals and police stations tend to dominate their lives which are anything other than tranquil. Violence, pain and heart-ache is no stranger to these leather clad men. Now, they are content to be sitting on a garden wall belonging to one of the village residents as they casually observe all that is going on around them. They are totally aware of the looks they are receiving from passing folk. They see it in the eyes of strangers, suspicion; fear; distain; dislike; resentment. A child draws near, possibly curious because they look different and apart. The three men smile at the little boy just as the mother hurriedly steps forward with a scowl on her face, to drag him away to a safer distance. The three men continue chatting and watching, amused by the antics of seagulls which are diving upon the unwary to successfully purloin chips, cakes, ice-cream. They are not fussy, if it's reachable, they will have it.

'Can somebody help me, please?' An elderly lady emerges from the cottage upon who's wall the three are siting. A few stop to look at the distressed lady, then pass on their way. The leather clad trio are on their feet, turning to see the owner of the voice.

'Please, I need help!' repeats the lady to the world in general.

'What's the problem,'

'Are you hurt?'

'How can we help?'

They have all spoken, one after the other. Folk are pausing to watch as the three menacing young men walk up the garden path and approach the elderly lady. They watch her lead the men into the cottage. They do nothing other than to gawp.

'It's my Whiskers,' says the lady as she leads the three men through her tiny, but neat, kitchen into a beautiful cottage garden at the rear.

'Your whiskers,' repeats the tall one. 'What's wrong with them?'

'No, not those whiskers, it's Whiskers, my cat. He's got himself stuck up that tree. How he ever got up there I cannot imagine. He's quite old now.' The lady is pointing into the leaves of a silver birch on the border of her garden. The three young men follow the direction in which she's pointing and immediately spot a rather large tabby cat looking down at them from a swaying branch about seven metres from the ground.

'Okay, I'll do this,' says the middle-sized man. 'Cup your hands, Shorty.' No further words are spoken, or required, as Shorty, the tallest of the three, enables Tom to reach the lowest branch. The rescue is effortlessly executed in less than three minutes as Tom releases an ungrateful Whiskers who quickly vanishes into the undergrowth of shrubs.

'You've scratched your hand, young man,' says the concerned lady. 'Come inside and let me take a look.'

'Actually, it was your Whiskers that did it, but don't worry, it's okay, I'll live,' replies Tom with a smile.

'Well, at least stay and have a cup of tea, I've got some fresh scones and cream.'

No further invitation is required. Soon, all four of them are seated at a circular metal table on the lady's patio, enjoying the delights of a cream tea. 'I see you are all bikers,' says the old lady as she pours the tea into her best china cups. 'Are you here just for the day?'

'That's right Ma-am, we rode down from Gloucester,' replies Shorty.

'I do envy you,' says the old lady wistfully. 'It has been a while since I was on the open road … I say, young man,' addressing herself to Lofty, who is in fact, the shortest of the three. 'if you don't mind me saying so, you're doing that all wrong. It's jam first, then the cream. You're in Cornwall now, not Devon.'

'What difference does it make?' responds Lofty as, to please the lady, he prepares the other half of his scone in the prescribed manner.

'None really,' replies the old lady with a grin. 'It's tradition, a way of making us a bit different to the Devon lot. Have you enjoyed your visit to our village?'

'Yes, it's been interesting,' replies Lofty. 'We were just thinking of moving on when you called for help. We're intending to ride up through Bodmin Moor.'

'That sounds lovely, you'll enjoy that,' replies the old lady. 'I haven't been up there since my husband passed on. Do you mind if I walk up the road with you? I would like to see your bikes.' With a grin, she goes on to say, 'I have something to show you.'

Half an hour later, having secured the cottage, the strange site of three black-leather-clad men escorting an elderly lady up the road between the souvenir shops catches the attention of many visitors. At the top of the climb, they lead the old lady to the three machines. She stands for a while, admiring them with obvious pleasure.

'I wish we could take you for a spin Mrs Kent, but the way you are dressed, and with no crash helmet, it just wouldn't be possible, even if you had wanted to.' says Tom.

'How kind,' replies the elderly lady. 'I said I've got something I want to show you, follow me.' With mystified looks between them, the three men follow the lady to a line of private garages to the side of the car park. Stopping in front of one of them and producing a key from the pocket of her jacket, she opens the double doors and stands back for the three friends to enter the space within.

'A Harley!' exclaims Tom.

'A Softail, I think,' says Shorty in awe.

'Wow,' says Lofty. 'Did this belong to your husband, Mrs Kent?'

'No dear, I sold his several years ago. This one is mine. I don't use it so much these days. I miss the company on the road,' replies the elderly lady while shaking her head.

'Can you still ride it?' enquires Tom.

'Oh yes, my gear is stowed in that cupboard over there in the corner. Last time out was two weeks ago. Just a few miles to keep the wheels turning for both me and the bike.'

'How do you feel about riding with us, up to the Moor?' asks Tom. We would be honoured and we'll get you back safely. You can trust us to take care of you. You see, we've been friends since school. Shorty here is a police officer, Lofty is a paramedic, and I'm a vicar. What could ever go wrong? Every possibility covered; you might say.'

'I would love to. I had hoped you might ask. I will try not to go too fast for you,' replies the elderly lady who is already removing her jacket.

The End

A Light Lunch

A narrow chink in the drawn curtain of the front room allows a little of the early morning light to creep into the room. Enough light, that is, to enable the crust, which is all that remains of a pizza, to be seen lying on the carpet beneath a coffee table. The coffee table must be assumed as, apart from the metal legs, it cannot be seen. It is there to be sure, although it is completely hidden by three wine bottles, one of which is a quarter full of red wine while its companions lie empty on their sides on the table. Also empty, apart from crusts and the smeared remains of various pizza toppings, are two dinner plates. The corner of an overfilled ash-tray is evident as it pokes out from beneath a Radio Time magazine. A TV remote sits on the open page of this magazine, as does a mobile phone which continues to vibrate, having done so for the last ten minutes.

A black and white cat silently enters the room and, disdainfully sniffs the pizza crust before effortlessly jumping onto the concealed coffee table where it licks the two plates before settling down on the Radio Times. Any chance of the absent mobile owner hearing the hum of the vibration is now non-existent. The chances of the owner hearing the vibrating phone was however, already non-existent, for on the first floor, immediately above the coffee table, she is lying face down beneath the covers of a king-size bed. Her clothes are scattered around the bedroom as are her husband's. Two empty wine glasses are standing on bedside cupboards on either side of the bed. She is aware of her husband's breathing, not a snore as such, more of a snort and a whistle. She is fortunately facing away from him, otherwise the retched man would be rudely awoken by a short, sharp jab in the ribs by a very pointy elbow.

She is sinking back into that blissful state of part-thought and part recovered dream, a rather nice one as it happens. The tall, elegantly dressed gentleman, in whose apartment she finds herself, escorts her to his grand piano where he gently removes the champaign glass from her beautifully manicured hands, sits her on the stool and, in the most romantic way, whispers in her ear, *'Play for me my sweet princess.'* She looks up into his deep blue eyes as she allows her fingers to gently caress the keys. The room is filled with the velvety sound of … *"My Old Man's a Dustman, 'e Wears a Dustman's Hat."* 'MY OLD MAN'S A

DUSTMAN? … George! GEORGE! Your mobile's ringing! Wake-up blast you!'

'What? Where?' The bed erupts as the quilt is thrown back by her husband who half rolls and half falls to the edge of the bed. 'Hello? Who is it? …. HELLO! … HELLO!'

'That's the TV zapper you're talking into, George,' says Tracey as the tune of *My Old Man's a Dustman* continues to fill the room.

'Oh, where's the blasted phone then? What time is it anyway?'

'It's eleven-fifteen, try looking under the bed, George,' replies an exasperated wife who, having glanced at the bedside clock, is quickly becoming aware of a headache coming on. 'And get that retched call sign changed.'

As suddenly as it started, the all-consuming and retched sound of old men and dustbins is replaced by George's shocked utterance of 'WHAT DO YOU MEAN, THE QUEEN'S COMING TO US FOR A LIGHT LUNCH? WHO IS THIS ANYWAY? … The Lord Chamberlain's office, now I know it's a wind-up.' He angrily presses the red phone symbol to end the call before throwing his mobile onto the bedside table.

'Who was that, George, and what do they want?' enquires Tracey. 'Oh, my poor head, and I've just remembered, today's the day we've arranged for my friend Queeny to come for lunch to meet your mate Foxy, it'll have to be burgers on the barby, we haven't got anything else in.'

'That was some crank who says the Queen is coming here for lunch today, says that she likes to pay a surprise visit to ordinary people now and then … as if.'

As Tracy slips on one of George's shirts before heading for the bathroom she grimaces and says, 'Well, we may not be entertaining the Queen but we have got Queeny and Foxy coming, so we need to get a move on.' As she reaches the door, the offending tune of *My Old man's a dustman* once again pierces her tender head. 'What now?' she demands as George fumbles to stop the offending noise.

'Yes, that's me. Who's calling please? Oh no, not you again, now listen … The Lord Chamberlain … I see, well I don't see actually … At twelve o-clock precisely … alone … discreetly …. informal … "Mam" as in "jam," then Your Majesty for the rest of the visit. Sir, Your Lordship, or whatever you are, do we have any choice in this? … I see … an honour … yes, I understand.

Oh, I've just remembered, we have friends coming round for lunch and … I see, just carry on as normal, that's the whole idea … best of lu … Hello? … HELLO? … Bloody hell!'

'Well, who was it that time?' enquires Tracey as she stands in the doorway sipping water from a tumbler with an open box of paracetamol tablets in her other hand.

'It was the Lord Chamberlain, the Queen really is coming here today for a light lunch, twelve o-clock, he said.'

'Pull the other one, who was it really?'

'Tracey, believe me, this is no joke, the Queen of England will be knocking on our front door in,' looking at the clock, 'ninety minutes time.'

'No!'

'Yes!'

'She can't be!'

'She can be … she is!'

'Oh my god! I must ring mother!'

'NO!!!!! That would be a disaster, five minutes with her and we'll all end up in The Tower.'

'Oh my god!'

'You've already said that, now what do we do?'

'Let me think …. You go down and sort out the kitchen and lounge, heaven knows how we left it all last night before you dragged me upstairs. I'll go and have a shower then see what's in the fridge beside burgers and that furry cheese.'

It's an hour later, and the kitchen and lounge are looking as tidy as can be expected, apart from the red wine stain in front of the cleared coffee table. The disgruntled cat, having been shoved out the back door, is hissing at George who has increased the cat's temper by sweeping him off the lid of the barbecue. 'Don't tempt me, Corky, we're desperately short of meat, good job we bought those cheap burgers from the market yesterday.'

He's having problems getting the coals to burn having forgotten to buy some fire-lighters after the last barby. He looks up as Tracey, now dressed as though she's about to descend a sweeping staircase to the applause of the other guests at the grand ball. 'Blimey, Trace, you sure that's suitable for a burger in our back yard?'

'Of course, it is,' she replies as she gives a twirl, narrowly missing the cat's gift which is simmering on the patio. 'Her Majesty's bound to be dressed up in her finery. Oh, by the way, Queeny has just phoned to say she can't come, something to do with her car being impounded. I warned her about sticking a blue light on top to get her kids to school on time in the mornings. Haven't you got that thing going yet? You've only got half an hour. I've managed to cut off the brown bits from the lettuce, and the cucumber's a bit on the soft side but passable. The buns are long passed their best but they'll have to do. Lots of tomato sauce will sort that.'

Half an hour later, with the barbecue producing more smoke than heat, the couple are peering through the net curtains with nervous expectation. 'Do you think she'll have a police escort and lots of staff?' Tracey wonders?

'Maybe a couple of outriders or something, it's supposed to be discreet, he said.' replies George. 'I wonder what's keeping Foxy, he's usually early where food's involved. I was hoping we could warn him to be polite and to watch his language. Hello, what's this coming up the road. Looks like a clapped-out Land Rover judging by the rust. Obviously looking for a parking space, glad

I put the dustbin out on the road to keep a space outside our house. Oh no, I do not believe it, he's reversing into our space. Look he's even shunting the bin out of the way with his rear fender. Cheek! I've a mind to … Hang on, it looks like an old man, although it could be a woman, hard to tell with those baggy trousers and raincoat on, and who wears sunglasses on a dull day like this? What's that he's reaching for? … A handbag. A HANDBAG!!!'

'A HANDBAG!' screams Tracey. 'It's her! Quick, open the front door, George before that nosey Mrs Death next door sees. She's bound to pop her head over the fence asking to borrow a cup of sugar once she knows who's here.'

'Oh, I say, what a charming house, and look at those delightful statues in the front garden, Mr & Mrs Bull I assume?'

'Gnomes, Mam.'

'Nomes? Not Bull?'

'That's right, gnomes, and yes, we are Mr & Mrs Bull, George and Tracey, Your Majesty. Please come in, mind the bike in the passage, I meant to put it in the garden before …'

‘Oh, how delightful, it must be simply *marvellous* to be able to ride such a machine. I get around by horse whenever I can, no peddles of course, otherwise just the same. Did you say “George”? We have had a few Georges in the family, you know.’

‘Would you like a cup of tea, Mam?’ asks Tracey.

‘That would be most acceptable, er …Tracey. What blends do you have?’

‘Co-op tea bags.’

‘My favourite,’ replies the gracious lady. ‘Can I be of any assistance in the kitchen? After all, you are hardly dressed for working in a kitchen, whereas ….’

‘Oh no, Your Majesty. Please go straight through to the yar … garden, George will lead you through. George, why don’t you show the Queen your barbecue?’

‘Certainly, this way Your Majesty.’ Conscious of the protocol of not turning one’s back to the queen, George steps backward through the back door and promptly discovers the wet gift left by Corky.

‘Oh, crap! I mean ...’

'Do not worry, George, I've stepped into turds bigger and wetter than that when spending time with my lovely horses. One simply must rub one's shoe or boot on the grass. Now, let us have a look at that barbecue, shall we? It's not looking too promising is it?'

It is fifteen minutes later that Foxy puts in an appearance, having walked around the side of the house directly into the back garden. By this time, Tracey has changed into jeans and a roll-neck jumper and has produced a mug of tea, not having found the china cup and saucer she was sure would be tucked away in the loft somewhere. The Queen in bending over the barbecue blowing onto the coals as though she's inflating a blow-up bed, the kind she keeps for Charles, should he decide to leave his farm and pay his parents a visit. She has soot on her nose and forehead as well as one cheek. George is still wiping his shoe on the small amount of grass the garden boasts.

'Hiya, everyone, sorry I'm late, got held up at the betting shop, placed a bet on the Queen's horse to win at the 3.30. Quite a nag, the horse I mean, although … Ah, looks like we're in for a barby, great, my stomach's been rumbling like an old lavatory. And this lady bending over the barby must be Queeny, a bit older than I was expecting, still, beggars can't be choosers, can they? Hiya luv, I like the make-up. I'm Foxy, pleased to meetcha.'

Startled by the sudden appearance of his friend, George quickly tries to stop Foxy before …

'Oh, I say!' says the Queen. 'Are you by any chance related to Lord Foxley who owns a large estate in Cumbria?'

'If only,' replies Foxy. 'No, my old man was a docky, and his dad before him. So, what do you do, Queeny, when you're not messing with barbecues?'

Clearly startled by this sudden turn of events, the Queen, with all her years of diplomacy behind her, regains control 'Oh, I travel a bit when not dealing with correspondence and wayward relatives, otherwise it's the horses that take much of my time, as well as the dogs.'

'I can see we are going to get on. Nothing I like better than a flutter on the 'orses and being down at the dog stadium with a giant size hot-dog on a Thursday evening. Looks like you've got the magic touch, luv, that barby is about ready for the tucker, speaking of which, here comes Tracey with the meat. What you got there then, Trace?'

'It's burgers I'm afraid. The best we could do at such short notice.' A meaningful glance at the Queen was fortunately unnoticed.

'Burgers!' exclaims the Queen, 'How delightful, one can become a little tired of stag when eating outdoors in Scotland, you know.'

'Got any beer, George? My throat's as tight as a cat's ...'

'YES! Foxy, in the fridge, why don't you pop in and help yourself?'

'Yea, I will, thanks. Do you want one, Queeny?'

'Yes please,' says the Queen, 'I haven't enjoyed a beer since my last trip on the yacht.'

'Wow! A yacht, you say, I love messing about on the water myself, I dare say you're a dab hand with the ropes and stuff …'

'Foxy, why don't you get those beers? There's a good chap.'

Soon the aroma and sizzle of barbecued burgers fills the senses as the Queen repeatedly turns the meaty discs over above the flames. Conversation becomes somewhat stilted until Foxy reappears carrying a tray of four bottles. He places the tray on the plastic patio table alongside a bowl of sorry-looking salad, then steps over to where the Queen is industrially cooking their lunch. Handing an opened bottle to the Sovereign he says, ‘Here you are, luv, get that down your gullet,’ then casually tips some beer onto his hanky before reaching forward with the wet cloth to wipe soot from her face. ‘You remind me of someone, Queeny, it’ll come to me in time, never forget a face.’

Not being able to endure further suspense, not to mention embarrassment, Tracey suddenly blurts out, ‘Foxy, this is the Queen.’

‘Yea, I know, you’ve been trying to get us together for months now, she’s okay, I like her. A bit old perhaps but on my wave length. What do you say Queeny? We could have a good time, eh?’

‘FOXY!!’ Interrupts George. ‘This is THE QUEEN. You know, as in “*My husband and I*”, Queen Elizabeth the second?’

Silence.

‘THE …Queen?’

‘Yes, Foxy,’ says Tracey. ‘Tell him Your Majesty.’

'A pity, I haven't had such a good time since my sister and I escaped from the palace for a while at the end of the war,' says the queen quietly. 'Perhaps, Tracey, you would be kind enough to fetch the buns, these burgers are ready.'

The party mood improves as burgers in buns are heartedly consumed. George and Tracey are relieved to see Foxy conversing politely with the Queen as they start to clear the plates prior to bringing out the yogurts, all they have to offer as a desert.

It's with a sense of relief a short while later when it becomes clear that the Queen is preparing to leave. 'Thank you so much,' she says as she struggles into her coat. 'I've had a lovely time and you have been so kind allowing me to come at so short a notice. I appreciate it.'

'It's been an honour Your Majesty. Drive carefully back to the palace,' says George.

'Oh no, George, Foxy and I are off to the betting shop to see how my horse is doing. I have got a thousand on it to win. If she comes in, who knows, how the day will end? Come along Foxy, we will take my car, it's seen better days but it will get us there.'

The End

The Runaways

It was now the third day. During the night the two children had had a more sheltered resting place than the previous one in which they had been forced to snuggle up together with nothing but their thin coats to cover them. It was fortunate that the ditch they had found was dry. Last night however had been more comfortable. They had come across an old barn at the edge of a field. Although it had been open sided there had been sufficient hay bales within to enable them to create a den in which they could find some warmth.

They were hungry. They had originally set out with the remains of a loaf and a small block of cheese. Their modest fare was augmented by two apples which they had managed to pick from a tree in their local church graveyard, aware that the workhouse warder may at that very moment be hammering at the door they had so recently closed for the last time. They had eaten the last of their food for breakfast, before reluctantly leaving the comparative safety of the barn. If they were to stay together, they knew that it would not be safe to linger in that area any longer than was necessary.

Day 3

The new day into which they had emerged from the barn gave them little encouragement to continue their journey. The sky was filled with scudding black clouds which totally hid the friendly warmth of the sun. Large drops of rain were splashing on their exposed heads as the children bent forward with hunched shoulders in a futile attempt to stay as dry as possible. As they left the field and struck out along a narrow muddy lane the older child, a twelve-year-old girl, took her brother's hand and gave it an encouraging squeeze. 'Come on Benny, you've been very brave and you're doing well. Can you see those woods ahead? If they go on for a long way the trees will help to keep us dry. We might find some nuts or blackberries, even some mushrooms.'

The seven-year-old boy was not so easily placated however, as he started crying and sniffing while rubbing his eyes with his free hand. 'Will we ever see mummy again, Flo? I want to go back to how it was before. Can we?'

'I'm sorry, Benny. We talked about this yesterday, remember? Mummy has died, the fever took her to heaven. That's where you will see her again, but it won't be for a long time. She asked you to be a good boy and to do what I tell you, even when you don't like it. We can't go back. The cottage isn't ours anymore and the people in the workhouse won't be kind to us. You remember, she gave me a letter to give to her sister, our aunty, we've never met her but she's bound to take care of us, you'll see. Now, wipe your nose and let's run so that we can get to those trees quicker.'

Day 1

'Gone! But they won't get far, you mark my words. They'll be heading for Portsmouth, I'll be bound. Where else would they go, eh?'

'I dunno sir,' replied the weaselly young clerk who was standing alongside his master Mr Scrim, while scratching his pimply nose. 'P'raps they'll try and get to Lunnon.'

'Idiot! And why, do you suppose, they would think they could walk that far? No, those juicy ripe children are going the other way, to the coast. Why am I even bothering to share my thoughts with you, one who's never had a thought in his life? Go back to the workhouse, Weasel, and tell Rose to get my horse saddled and to be sure to put some food and cider in the bag. I'll be back there in half an hour after I've had a last look around this miserable home, they've felt fit to leave.'

Day 2

The rotund warder had now spent two days in frustration, not having had sight or sound of the runaway children. None that he had spoken to had been able to help, although he suspected they were unlikely to do so even if they could. His growing frustration was exacerbated by Weasel's inability to keep up as he stumbled alongside the horse upon which he himself had sat throughout the two-day search.

'Bah! I felt sure those two vermin would have come this way,' exclaimed Scrim. 'Portsmouth was the most obvious place to go. You can't trust anyone to do what they should. We'll lodge in The Post Inn in Petersfield tonight. I'm sure they can put you up in the stable, Weasel.'

'Thank you kindly, Mr Scrim, you're always so thoughtful. Do you think they might have headed for Lunnon after all, Mr Scrim?'

'If you mention London once more, Weasel, I'll not be responsible for my actions, and stop scratching that overgrown nose of yours. Idiot!'

Day 3

The rain, if anything, had fallen more heavily before the children had reached the comparative shelter of the woods. As water had started to cascade down the rutted lane Florence had decided that it would be wise to climb the mossy bank and try to stay as dry as possible under the mixed canopy of oak, elm, and chestnut. As they made their way through the trees, parallel with the lane, they foraged for blackberries and even managed to find some prickly chestnuts lying open on the ground, although Benny complained about the bitter taste once they had managed to split open the glossy inner shells of a few of them.

The children, once secure with their mother, a school teacher, in the warm comfort of their cosy home, a rented cottage in a small hamlet, were now cold, hungry, grief-stricken, and afraid. If it were possible, they would be even more afraid had they been aware of a pair of glinting eyes watching their every movement. The wet morning gave way to a gloomy afternoon during which the rain had ceased. It was the waterlogged canopy that now kept dripping onto the children and the hidden watcher.

'How do you know we're going the right way, Flo?' enquired the tearful boy as the enormity of the situation in which they found themselves threatened to bring on a panic attack. 'I know you've never been this far from home before and these woods are creepy. What if a big bear jumps out at us?'

'There aren't any bears here, big or small, Benny. The only animals we're likely to see are deer and squirrels, you like those don't you?'

'Yes, but you still haven't told me how you know where we are.'

'Well, we are still close to the lane, and that will lead to a main road where we can ask for directions to Guildford. Who knows? We might even get a ride on a cart, or something. Come on, let's see if the lane's a bit better now.'

Had it not been for the disturbance of the breeze rustling the undergrowth they may not have been quite so shocked when each of them felt a hand suddenly rest on their shoulders.

'Well, well, well, what have we here? Two little children lost in the woods, is it?' Both screamed. Before either of them had a chance to run, the gnarled hands gripped their shoulders like a vice.

'Let me go!' bellowed Benny whilst Florence continued to scream.

'Quiet! You'll disturb the game,' A sharp reprimand indeed. 'Stop that screaming, girl!' The authoritative voice was that of a woman, although barely more than a loud whisper. 'I won't harm you. You have nothing to fear from me, little ones. Are you hungry?'

For Benny, the word "hungry", at that moment, dominated his fear. He swung round to peer into the kindly face of a late middle-aged woman.

'Thought so. Starving if my intuition serves me right.'

As Florence drew breath for another scream, the word *starving* infiltrated her panicked brain. She also turned to face her captor who now smiled at her, a gap in her front teeth very prominent.

'Let's see,' said the woman as she raised her eyes to the wet canopy above. 'You have a choice. You can leave these woods on that lane yonder, or you can come with me to my comfy little hut where I have a nice rabbit stew simmering over hot ashes. It's up to you my luvvies, but I know what I would do.' By this time, although neither of the children had noticed, she had removed her hands from their shoulders and had placed both on the knob of a carved stick which had been leaning against her leg.

'Keep up, you overgrown lump of lard. We've already wasted too much time on that Portsmouth road. At this rate we'll never catch the wretches.' Master and servant had returned to the workhouse for a rest and were now headed in the opposite direction toward London. Scrim was secretly doubting that they would ever find the runaways now, but for the sake of his reputation not to mention his job, he had to at least show the trustees of the workhouse that he had made every reasonable effort.

‘I see from that milestone back there that we’re on the Lunnon road now Mister Scrim,’ said Weasel. ‘Should ‘ave done that in the first place, if you ask me.’

‘Shut your mouth, Weasel, get a move on before I take this cane to your miserable backside. Nobody wants your opinion, least of all, me.’ With that disdainful comment Scrim dug his heels into the tired horse’s ribs and flicked the reins in order to put him on the trot. ‘Move yourself, Weasel,’ he shouted over his shoulder.

The two children had followed the woman deeper into the woods. Although nervous of the new development, Florence had come to the decision that they would have to trust the strange woman, for they had been wet through to the skin as well as extremely cold and hungry. It was therefore with a sense of relief and delight when they had their first glimpse of the hut to which she had referred. It was set in a clearing amongst the trees and seemed to be made of clay and wood, with a roof of branches and fern-like greenery. It even boasted a doorway which was screened with sacking. Alongside the hut was a small three-sided screened area in which a fireplace was evident by the thin trickle of smoke rising through a roof of greenery into the overhanging bushes. The children had little opportunity to survey the site as the old lady quickly hustled them into the dark interior of the hut which they found surprisingly warm.

'You two get out of that wet clothing and wrap these blankets around you while I see to the fire,' said the woman. 'We'll soon have some warming stew in your stomachs. You can call me Bell, what's your names?'

Florence spoke for both of them as she helped her little brother out of his soggy breeches. 'This is my brother, Benny, and I'm Florence but everyone calls me Flo. We are orphans and are on our way to our aunties house in Guildford.'

'So, it's Guildford you'll be heading for. Just as well I saw you, for you were heading in the wrong direction. It's the London road you'll be wanting to travel. Best you stay here for the day, to dry out those clothes and feed yourselves up. You can leave in the morning. After you've eaten you can tell me all about yourselves.'

The woman had patiently listened to their story and learned of a caring widowed mother who had worked in their local school in order to shelter, cloth and feed her two children. How their mother had seldom spoken about her sister. How the children's mother had been taken by a fever only two days after complaining of feeling unwell. How the local magistrate had organised the funeral and for the children to be taken into care.

Bell had remained silent throughout the sorry tale, just an occasional grunt, or nod, to indicate that she was still listening. The telling of the story was not without tears from both children, and, once or twice, their new friend gave a loud sniff as she sucked on a foul-smelling clay pipe.

With the story told, right up to the point where she had first spoken to them, Bell said, 'You poor, poor mites. So young to be looking for an aunty you've never met, in the hope she will take you in.'

'Oh, but she *must!'* exclaimed Florence. 'Why would she *not* do that? She's our only living relative, she *has* to … doesn't she?'

'Tell me, child when did your dear mother last see her sister, do you know?'

'Not really,' replied Florence. 'I think it was just before Benny was born. Daddy had been lost at sea and Mummy needed help as she had to stop working. I know she sent a letter because she kept the reply for a while. I think I was too young to understand why aunty didn't come. Anyhow, I have a new letter for Aunt Mabel that Mummy wrote the day before she died, I've kept it safely tucked into my drawers. Would you like to see it?'

'No, my dear. That's private, between two sisters,' replied Bell with a shake of her head. 'Now, I need to go out for a while. You two, stay here while your clothes are drying. You can put some logs on the fire if you want to feel more warmth, the dry ones are stacked over there in the corner. I shouldn't be too long. Roast rabbit tonight, I think.'

And so, it had turned out. Still not quite understanding how it was that they were sitting in a hut in the woods, wearing nothing but damp underclothes and blankets, they waited for the woman's return. It seemed a long wait but they felt safe enough knowing that they were free to walk away whenever they wanted. Bell eventually returned with two dead rabbits tied to a pole which she held over her stooped shoulder. Seeing that the children had dressed she allowed them to assist her with the preparation of supper, with Benny tending the fire as well as foraging for blackberries, while Florence gathered and prepared some wild mushrooms. The rabbits, having been skinned by Bell, were soon roasting on a carved wooden spit.

Stomachs satisfied, the three of them sat before the fire as the light faded, listening to the rustling of leaves in the trees and the evening song of a nearby blackbird. When asked by Florence how she had ended up living in the woods Bell sat back and looked up into the fading light of the canopy and simply responded with the word, "Contentment." Beyond that, she would say nothing.

That night, sister and brother settled on a bed of straw within the hut and, for a while, listened to the mysterious night noises of unseen creatures moving through the undergrowth, before eventually giving way to sleep in each other's arms. For a long time, Bell sat in the darkness by the embers of the fire thinking about the children and their story and what she intended to do in the morning.

Day 4

It took Florence a while to work out where she was, as sleep gave way to wakefulness the following morning. Benny was still soundly asleep with his head resting on her chest. She became aware of the pleasing sound of the dawn chorus, although it was not as loud as that experienced back at the cottage. She also became aware of the rustling trees and the smell of woodsmoke. Not wanting to disturb Benny, she remained still and allowed her mind to run over the experiences of the last few days. She thought about the friendly, but strange, woman who called herself Bell. Why was she living in this way? Why was she so willing to help two strange children? The more she allowed these questions to dominate her thoughts the more she wanted to know about her. She really wanted to trust Bell, but there was a lingering feeling of uncertainty. Frowning, she looked at the bedding that Bell had settled in last night. Not only was it empty but Florence came to the realisation that she had not heard the woman moving about since she herself had awoken. It was therefore with a sense of relief that Benny started to stir.

Had Florence been able to see Bell at that moment she would certainly have had great cause for concern. An observer would have seen her standing at a crossroads on the London road talking to a well-built man while handing him a small pouch.

By the time Bell had returned to the hut both children were dressed and had even managed to wash their faces in a nearby brook where they had seen her collecting water the previous day. She was pleased to see that Florence had built up the fire, although it took her a while to spot Benny who was sitting astride the branch of an oak tree, some twelve feet above the ground.

'Good morning children, I see you slept well, now I think it's time for breakfast before we leave. I have some herbs that will make us a nice warm drink, and we have some dry biscuits we can dunk into it.'

'Where have you been, Bell? We've been up for ages and were becoming concerned about what we should do. We didn't like to just walk off without thanking you.'

'Never you mind about what I've been doing, dear. We have no time for idle chat, as we must be on our way. There is much to be done today.'

'You say, "We" do you mean that you are coming to show us safely to the London road?'

'You'll see soon enough, but yes, we are all leaving together. I think this water is hot enough for the brew now.' Had the children known about the well-built man that Bell had spoken to, and that he was at that moment riding his horse along the London road, the same road that also leads to Petersfield and Portsmouth, the direction in which he was heading, they most certainly would not have stayed for a brew.

‘Keep your eyes pinned, Weasel. If the brats have come this way and should they see or hear us coming they’ll, no doubt, leave the road. This is the last day we can spare and I want those beauties very much …oh so very much. I’ll teach them not to waste my time, see if I don’t.’ With Weasel panting alongside the horse, Scrim took a swig of cider and wiped his thick wet lips on the arm of his, not too clean, coat. He continued his gaze ahead in the hope of seeing the children before they saw him, that is, assuming they were obligingly walking this road. Enquiries of the few folks they had passed on the road had failed to give him encouragement. By his pocket-watch he could see that they had been travelling for over two hours since they had left a mean roadside Inn that morning.

‘Mr Scrim! … Mr Scrim, wake up! I can see a rider up ahead. He’s coming this way.’

Scrim jumped with the realisation that he had indeed been guilty of allowing his eyes to close just for a moment. He had slept very little at the flea-ridden Inn. 'Do not assume that I was asleep, you oaf. I was waiting to see how long it would take you to spot the man, and it was too long. Now let us see if this gentleman has any news of wayward children, shall we?'

'Good morrow to you, Sir,' greeted the rider as he drew level. I see from your uniform that you are a man of certain responsibilities, may I enquire as to your occupation?'

'You may, good fellow. I am Mr Scrim, the chief warder of the Bordon workhouse. I am currently engaged in the search for two escapees. You wouldn't perchance have seen two children along this road? A girl with her young brother. Always causing trouble, those two.'

'This is indeed fortunate, Sir, for you are the very man I have been sent to find. I have within my saddlebag a pouch which may very well interest you.'

'But who? How ...?'

'I am not at liberty to say anything further, Sir. I suggest you take the pouch, which may provide a few answers. Now, if you will excuse me, I must bid you good day.'

The London road turned out to be closer than Florence expected. They had followed a well beaten track through the trees, keeping up with Bell who was walking faster than her age would suggest. As they emerged from beneath the canopy the children were startled to see a horse and trap standing at the crossroads. The driver, standing by the horse's head, had clearly been awaiting their arrival.

'Good!' said Bell as she turned to face the children. 'This kind man is going to take you to Guildford. You can trust him. Tonight, he will see that you have a comfortable place to stay, and in the morning, he will take you to your aunt's address. Have you got that letter in a safe place, Florence?'

'Yes, Bell. I checked it was there just before we left. I don't understand. How have you managed to get this man …'

'Thomas.'

'Thomas, to take us on our journey?'

'God moves in mysterious ways, child. Best you don't know. Now then, up you get, and remember, I'll always be your crazy old friend. Goodbye.' Turning from the bewildered children, the woman said, 'Okay, Thomas, you know what to do.' Having settled in the trap, the children turned to wave to their friend, but she was gone.

Day 5

It was on the following day that Florence stood at the large oak door, holding Benny's hand, waiting expectantly for someone to respond to the ringing of the bell. She had pulled on the chain a second time when the door swung open to reveal a smartly turned-out maid.

'I heard the first time, no need to keep ringing. What do you want? The mistress doesn't give to charity if that is why you're here.'

'Oh, no. You don't understand, she's our aunty. I have a letter for her,' replied a flustered Florence. 'Here.' With that, she reached beneath her coat and withdrew a badly crumpled envelope which she handed to the reluctant maid who sniffed and turned up her nose before gingerly taking the article between her fingers.

'Wait here.' The door closed behind her as she disappeared inside the three-story terraced house which overlooked the river.

'I didn't like her,' said Benny, 'and I don't like this house either.'

'Hush, Benny. She's just the maid. It will be alright once she tells Aunt Mabel who we are, you'll see.'

The nervous children were kept waiting outside the door for five minutes before it was re-opened. It was the maid again. 'The mistress says she doesn't know you and that you are to be gone. She won't see you.'

'I don't understand,' said Florence. 'Did you give her the letter?'

'Yes, I did. The mistress read it before she threw it on the fire. Now, be off with you before I fetch the constable.'

'But, she's our aunty. How can she not want to see us?'

'An aunty when it suits you, I dare say,' scoffed the maid. 'You're wasting your time, and mine, go away and don't come back.' The door was then slammed in their faces.

'I said I didn't like it here,' whined Benny. 'What can we do now?'

'I don't know, Benny. I'll think of something.' Both were in tears as they emerged from the front gate onto the pavement. For the first time since their mother had died Florence was at a total loss as to what to do next. It was at that moment that the familiar horse and trap pulled into the kerb beside them.

'Okay, kids. Hop in. I assume she doesn't want to help you. I was waiting just up the road to be sure.' Thomas waited until they were both seated, before flicking the reins and clicking at the horse.

'Where are you taking us?' asked Florence.

'Where you should have gone in the first place if you ask me. They will no doubt be expecting you. More than that, I cannot say.'

Day 6

It was late in the afternoon of the following day that the frightened children stepped down from the trap at the front of a large house which was hidden behind a high wall. ‘Okay, kids,’ said Thomas as he dismounted. ‘Follow me round the side.’ Soon they were standing in a long hallway and were not at all certain what they should do next. ‘Follow me, this way.’ Thomas led them along the passage to a flight of stone steps with iron railings. At the top, they followed him through a door and, to their amazement, found themselves in a beautifully furnished room with many paintings hung on the walls and with large draped windows overlooking a garden with a large fountain in the centre. Thomas indicated a sofa beside a carved stone fireplace, saying, ‘Please sit here while I fetch the mistress.’

‘This doesn’t look much like a workhouse from what I’ve heard,’ said an awe-struck Benny. ‘Where are we, Flo? And who’s the mistress he’s gone to fetch?’

‘I don’t know, Benny. I’m as confused as you are.’

‘I’m hungry. Do you think they’ll feed us before we have to go?’

‘Certainly, we will feed you, Benny.’

Startled by the silent entry, as well as the familiar voice, both of them leapt to their feet to be greeted by the sight of Bell. Only it wasn't Bell. This was a smartly dressed lady with Bell's face and Bell's warm smile.

'Bell?' asked Florence uncertainly.

'The very same, child. Well, not quite the same, as you see.'

'Why is Bell dressed like that, Flo? She looks pretty.'

'Why thank you, Benny. That is a nice thing to say,' responded Bell. The truth is, this is what I usually look like, except for my special times when I can spend a week or two out in the wild, my favourite place.'

'Do you mean, …' chipped in Florence, 'that you live here in this house?'

'Not only do I live here, Florence, I own it, and the woods in which I found you.'

'Gosh!' exclaimed Benny while looking around the room before stepping over to the window. 'Do you own that garden, and the fountain?'

'All of it, but my little hut in the woods is best,' Turning to Florence, Bell enquired, 'I assume your aunt in Guildford didn't want to know you, is that right?'

'She told her maid not to let us in.'

'As I thought. Well, children, I want you to stay here with me for as long as you like. I took the precaution of ensuring that the workhouse warder will never bother you again.'

'But, how did you do that?' asked Florence.

'Shall we say that he is a little better off right now? I also took the precaution of preparing bedrooms for you. I think you will like them. Now, let us go to the dining room and see what Cook has prepared for you. She has been so excited with the thought of having children in the house to fuss over. After you have eaten, I'll show you round your new home, should you decide to stay.'

The children lived in the manor for the remainder of their lives. They very quickly grew to love Bell, and she returned that love without reservation. A love that was to extend to Flo and Benny's own children as time passed.

Although brother and sister, and their children, loved the manor house, their favourite place on the whole estate was the little hut where they spent many happy times with their eccentric adopted mother and grandmother, who's presence always seemed so near amongst the trees long after her life ended at a ripe old age.

The End

The Ferryman

The old man paused for a moment before he was ready to share his thoughts. 'The Gap has a reputation, you know? Locals will tell you that it's not a place for the feint-hearted. Neither is it a place for any but the most experienced to venture out on. Along with its reputation is the tally. A tally of the lives it has ended. Young, old, strong, frail, it takes no heed. For it's hungry, always hungry for its next victim. It doesn't mind waiting for a bit, for it knows that the hunger will be satisfied soon or later, but never satisfied for long. It lives and breathes today, just as it did before man ever passed by, or settled in this place.' The old man shook his head as he glanced over the side of the boat into the swirling current.

Satisfied that he had the full attention of his only passenger, the *celebrity* who was grasping the seat upon which she sat, he continued, 'Needs to be said, as fearsome as it is, The Gap is a provider. It protects the inner basin, once a beautiful home for all manner of fish and fowl, today a natural harbour in which folk can enjoy the water in comparative safety. Many homes have been built along the shoreline of the harbour over the years, although there are a number of surviving woodlands and meadows running down to the water's edge, sufficient to maintain the beauty of the natural harbour. There's a narrow road skirting the harbour, well more of a lane, I suppose. By motorcar, the lane will take you as much as an hour to travel to the village of Dun over there on the south side from the town of Dunmore where I picked you up just now. That hour includes the narrow streets of Colmington at the head of the harbour. On foot, the journey will take a fit person the best part of a day. By horse and cart …well, nobody does that anymore, except old farmer Stubbs, and he doesn't go all the way round, no need, you see.'

For a while the old man paused in his narrative. The creaking of the oars in the rowlocks and the constant swirling of the racing water, the only sound. 'I said that The Gap is a provider. So, it is. As well as providing protection for the harbour it also provides this narrow crossing point to save the journey from Dun to Dunmore. There lies the danger. Many have tried to cross this half-mile wide gap in their little boats, or even by swimming, damn fools. Most have succeeded, but many haven't' The old man stopped talking for a while, he suddenly looked sad. His stroke on the oars however, didn't falter as he silently gazed at the water. There was barely a splash as he continued dipping the blades into the surface.

'The Gap is my friend. It respects me, as long as I respect its unwritten rules. It's provided me, and my family before me, with a living through the generations, and may well do so for my remaining son and his son. You see? I'm the Ferryman.'

The *celebrity* was sitting on the seat at the back of the large rowing boat which, she estimated, could seat up to five other passengers. To say she was happy and comfortable with the journey across The Gap would have been untrue. She was a little bit scared if the truth be told. She had noticed how small and vulnerable the ferry boat was as it had made its way across the fast-moving water to pick her up some half hour ago. Apart from that, the ferryman's comments about The Gap, was, to say the least, unsettling. She was comforted with the thought that she would not have to return to Dunmore in this rowing boat at the end of the ceremony. In order to take her mind off the crossing she said, 'I assume most of your passengers are regulars?'

'Well, my dear, it all depends on the time of year. In the winter, it's mostly regulars going over to do a bit of shopping or to go to a medical appointment or something. Come the spring, we start getting the day-trippers, then in the summer months it's the holiday makers, although they mostly like to drive their motorcars around the bay to get to the other side.'

'I suppose you know the regulars very well,' suggested the *celebrity.*

'Oh, yes. When I'm not out on the water I can usually find something to do to help the local folk, a bit of gardening or fetching, maybe a bit of painting or repair work. I don't charge of course, just doing what any neighbour would do.'

After thinking about the old man's last statement for a while, the *celebrity* asked, 'I don't want to seem as though I'm probing, and don't answer if you don't want to, but just now, you mentioned your remaining son. I assume from that, that you had another son. What happened to him?'

For a while the ferryman continued rowing in thoughtful silence, keeping up the rhythm of his work, occasionally glancing over his left shoulder to check his direction. Just as the *celebrity* began to think she had overstepped the mark he quietly said, 'He was one of those who, with his friend, thought he could swim across The Gap on an outgoing tide. We never found him. Just sixteen. Did it as a dare, apparently. They found his friend four days later, washed up along the coast several miles away.'

There was silence for a few moments, then, 'I'm sorry, please forgive me for asking,'

'It's okay, been a couple of years now. I'm mostly over it, but it killed his mother, my lovely wife Clare. She couldn't live with it. Never wanted to look at the sea again.'

'I'm so sorry …How old is your other son?'

'Fourteen. A sensible lad. He wants to take over from me at the end of his schooling. I had intended going on till then but arthritis has made it more and more difficult for me to row. I've loved this life, the sea, the elements, the folk who rely on me, even the holiday makers out to have a good time. Unfortunately, this is my last day. I respect The Gap too much to take the risk of rowing passengers across when no longer fit enough to do so. Don't know what I'll do after, just have to wait and see.'

Ten minutes later, as the small wooden pier in Dun drew closer, the ferryman asked, 'We don't get too many *celebrities* in these parts. What sort of ceremony are you doing over here? I haven't heard anything about a ceremony and I'm usually the first to know what's going on.'

'I'm sorry,' replied the *celebrity*. 'I've been sworn to secrecy, but you will find out soon enough, I can see folk are standing by the pier and waving. Looks like there expecting me.'

'I'll be ready to row you back, just as soon as you've finished your business. Hope it goes well, whatever it is.'

'Oh, I'm sure it will,' replied the *celebrity* with a smile. 'Thank you for sharing your story with me.'

The moment the ferryman tied his old rowing boat to a bollard, the vicar, Reverend Chalmers, in dog-collar and best suit stepped forward to help the *celebrity* step ashore. Having introduced himself he led the *celebrity* to a small table on which a large number of bottles and glasses were displayed, the whole time chatting to his guest. Soon everyone was holding a glass of bubbly wine in their hands, apart from the children who had beakers of orange squash.

'Ladies and gentlemen, friends and children, I have great pleasure in introducing Dame Cynthia Fielding, the well know singer. She has graciously made the crossing from Dunmore where she has been performing in The Regency Theatre during the autumn season, in order to present a gift to one of our best-known friends and neighbour. Throughout his life he has served this community in all weathers, both good and bad, not only in carrying out his duties but also to bring light into the lives of most of us. You may not know, because he never complains, that his rowing boat has made its last crossing, as his health makes it difficult for him to continue battling that current in The Gap. I am, of course referring to our much loved and appreciated ferryman, John Wilkins. Will you come forward, please, John?'

As the stunned ferryman stepped over to where the guest of honour and the reverend were standing, the whole assembly applauded and loudly cheered. Holding up her hands to quieten the crowd, Dame Cynthia addressed the old man, saying, 'John, it has been a great privilege to have been the last passenger in your rowing boat and to meet you. It is now my privilege to hand you the keys of your new powered boat which is, at this moment, being towed around the corner over there.' Pointing to the corner around which a tractor pulling a trailer was emerging on cue, she smiled at the astonished old man. 'The community you have loved and served for so many years have clubbed together to purchase this gift. It will soon be my privilege to be the first passenger on your brand-new motor boat, and I am so happy to have a nice cosy cabin to sit in on the way back to Dunmore. And now, you may want to inspect your smart motor-boat and supervise her launching.'

The End

Boy Meets Girl

Slowly, Luke walked away from the house in which he had spent the evening. It had not been planned. It wasn't as though he had intended to come between his best friend and Lucy. It was just a chance encounter. His mind took him back to his visit to the Saturday market down in the High Street that morning. Not knowing where his mate Frank was, he had gone into town alone. He had been on the lookout for any old vinyl records that featured his favourite guitar player, Duane Eddy. He had hopefully thumbed through various boxes before re-checking, in case he had missed something. Aware of the suspicious glances he was receiving from the stall holder he had eventually given up and turned to walk away. Having emerged from beneath the stall's canvas cover he had been surprised to find that the intensity of his search had hidden from him the fact that it was now raining. With hunched shoulders and head hidden by his hoody, Luke attempted to dodge the forest of umbrellas as he dejectedly headed for the bus stop at the end of the precinct. *No point in hanging around here now. Might as well head for home.* He remembered that there was to be a snooker match on the telly during the afternoon and that his father was sure to be watching it. *Might as well sit with him and try to understand what it's all about.* Luke was not a follower of snooker. Cricket for sure, tennis sometimes, but snooker? *A bit slow if you ask me.*

Emerging from Debenhams, Lucy had promptly pressed the button that would raise her umbrella, before stepping carefully around the puddles as best she could, given that there were so many shoppers hurrying passed. Her intention was to call into the book shop on the opposite side of the precinct before heading for home.

After two people had already carelessly bumped into her, she was rather annoyed when a third person did the same. 'Sorry,' an exasperated voice came from somewhere within a hoody.

'You should look where you're going. You nearly made me drop my bag!' Lucy complained, rather loudly.

'I said, I'm sorry. What more do you want? Anyhow, you weren't looking where you were going with that umbrella hiding your face,' retorted Luke.

Indignantly, Lucy moved the umbrella to one side so that she could look at the offensive young man who was still hidden beneath the hoody. 'Well, you can't speak, you definitely can't see anything except your own feet from beneath that hood. Come out and apologies properly.' With a shrug of the shoulders, Luke removed his hands from his pockets and swept back the hoody. 'Luke? You're Frank's friend. I thought your voice was vaguely familiar. Fancy bumping into you!'

'Oh, so now you admit that it was you that bumped into me,' replied Luke with a grin. 'Yea, I'm Luke and now I can see that your Frank's girlfriend. Lucy, isn't it?'

'Yes, that's right,' replied Lucy. 'We've been going out for three months now, but I expect you know that.'

'Well, I knew it was a while. Is Frank down here with you? I called for him but was told he's out with someone.'

'No,' replied Lucy with a frown. 'I haven't seen him since last Sunday.'

'Look, we're both getting wet,' said Luke, who suddenly wanted to prolong the encounter. 'Do you fancy a burger or something?'

'Okay, how about Burger King? It's the closest one.'

That is how it all started. They had taken their time eating lunch, for they both found they were enjoying each other's company. They discovered that they had much in common in respect of music and television programme preferences. Lucy particularly liked Luke's dry sense of humour. Most of all, she was flattered that he seemed to be genuinely interested in her thoughts and ambitions. As for Luke, he found that he was enchanted by the fact that Lucy could smile while eating, smile while talking, and smile as she listened to him. One subject that did not crop up was Luke's best friend, Frank. One hour passed in a flash, then two slipped by as the young couple lost themselves in shared attraction.

A short while after the second hour, a staff member approached and asked them if they required any further food or drink. It was only then that Luke noticed other customers who were waiting for a table. 'A polite way to say "On your bike," he said with a grin, as he rose to his feet.

'I didn't notice how much time had passed,' replied Lucy as she slipped into her coat. 'What are you doing now?' she enquired.

‘Nothing much. I was here looking for a Duane Eddy record but no luck. What about you?’

‘I’m going home now. I don’t suppose you would like to come back to my house, would you? I have got a few Duane Eddy records, and The Shadows. We could listen to those, but only if you want to.’

‘Sounds good to me. So, you’re not meeting Frank then?’

‘Nothing planned,’ replied Lucy. ‘Let’s go, my parents won’t mind you coming round, I’m sure.’

The afternoon spent in Lucy’s bedroom had been exciting, confusing, and, if Luke really thought about it, a little worrying. For he had found that he was becoming attracted to Lucy, his best friend’s girl. Every so often, her mum or dad had popped their heads around the door to ensure that all was well. Following an invitation from Lucy’s mother, Luke phoned to let his mum know where he was, and that he was staying for the evening meal. After the meal of stew and dumplings, the table cleared, and washing up done by the youngsters, the couple joined Lucy’s parents in the lounge where they were allowed to occupy the sofa while watching a film on the television. The lights had been dimmed for the film so her parents didn't notice that the youngsters were holding hands during most of the film.

As he walked the relatively short distance home at the end of the evening, Luke reminded himself again that none of this had been planned. It would never have been his intention to fall in love that day, or any other day soon, as far as he was concerned. But to fall in love with his best friend's girl was something else. He and Frank had been best mates for as long as he could remember. They shared everything, but sharing a girl was definitely off the chart. It was clear that she liked him. Even her parents seemed to accept him. It was Lucy whose idea it was to meet again tomorrow. At the time, he jumped at the chance, but now? He wasn't so sure that it would be a good idea. *Frank's my best mate, he trusts me. He will never speak to me again. Might even give me a good thumping. What am I doing?*

'Is that you, Luke?'

Cripes, who else would it be? 'Yes mum, just putting the kettle on.'

'Make one for us then, there's a luv.'

Luke's parents were sitting in the lounge, dad reading a paper, mum quietly knitting. The radio was tuned to classical music as Luke entered with the tray of mugs.

'Had a good day, son?' enquired his dad as he folded up the paper and stoked his pipe.

'Yea, met up with a friend and spent the rest of the day at her home.'

'On the phone, you said her name was Lucy,' piped in his mum. 'That wouldn't be Frank's girlfriend by any chance, would it?'

'Yes.'

'I see,' she said while putting down her knitting to lift one of the mugs of tea. 'Speaking of Frank, he called round this afternoon, looking for you. He had a girl with him. Jenny, I think her name was. Do you know her?'

'No, I don't think so.'

'Well,' said his dad as he drew on the pipe to get it started. 'He seemed to know her quite well, I noticed they were holding hands as they walked down the road together. She seemed a bit older than Frank, at least thirteen, possibly even fourteen. Do you still want me to help you with that Meccano tomorrow, son?'

‘No thanks, dad,’ replied the grinning boy. I’m meeting Lucy.’

The End

A Right Royal Birth

'Mrs Trent?'

'Yes, I'm ready. In fact, more than ready.'

Glancing down at the rounded tummy of his passenger the taxi driver gulped before replying, 'Yea, I can see that, misses. Looks like you're nearly due. Going in for a check-up, are you?'

'No. In fact you might say this is something of an emergency. My waters broke half an hour ago, you see. It could come any time now. How quickly can you get me to the hospital?'

'Half an hour if I put my foot down, and believe me, misses, my foot's gonna go down very hard. These your bags to go?'

'Yes,'

'Right then, give 'em to me, I'll take 'em while you lock up.'

So it was that Clare Trent, holding her protruding tummy beneath her un-buttoned overcoat, stepped down the front garden path, oblivious to the twitching net curtains of more than one front room close by.

And so it was, that Lenny Stagg's day changed from the normal routine of a city cab driver to one he would never, for the remainder of his life, forget. As it turned out, a few other people, for various connected reasons, also had cause to remember that sunny spring day.

Clare and her husband were tenants in a small damp terraced house which was owned by a private landlord who could never be accused of being over-zealous in his ideas of property maintenance. They had been married nine months ago and, on a self-employed window cleaner's income, couldn't afford to be too fussy in their selection of affordable accommodation. According to the notes, their bundle of joy was not expected until the following week, so the breaking of her waters as she was washing-up the breakfast dishes had been a bit of a shock for Clare. Now, as she sat in the back of the cab with her birthing bag alongside her, she tried once again, without success, to ring her husband on her mobile.

Lenny Stagg carefully pulled away from the curb, having waited patiently for a cyclist to pass. Glancing into his internal mirror he could see his passenger tapping numbers into her mobile before holding it to her ear. She looked calm enough, so nothing to worry about. His half-hour estimate was meant to reassure the young lady, whereas the reality was most likely going to be at least forty minutes, if he was lucky. Easing his cab onto the main road he thought back to the birth of his first nipper, a boy. A home birth that disallowed him to stay in the room as his son bawled his way into the world. Eighteen months later, he had missed the birth of his daughter at the hospital by just ten minutes. He had been looking forward to that magical moment, seeing her come into the world and into their lives. Good kids, they had been, now young adults making their way in the world.

Five minutes into the journey, all going well. His passenger had given up on her mobile. 'You all right, Luv?' he enquired as he glanced briefly into his mirror.

'Yes, but can you go faster? The pains have started.'

'Crickey!'

'It's okay, but best not to hang around.'

'Believe me, luv, I'm not intending to hang around, This your first?'

'Yes. My mum was always fast giving birth to me and my four brothers, runs in the family, she says.'

'Blimey!'

A minute later, Lenny slowed down as he approached the end of a stationery queue of traffic. Trying to peer round the cars ahead he could see no obvious cause for the hold-up. With his thumbs tapping a tattoo on the steering wheel Lenny fumed as the car ahead moved forward a matter of five metres before the break lights came on again. One minute became two, then three. It seemed more like ten to the frustrated taxi driver. He wondered if he could manage a U-turn and had just shifted into reverse gear to allow more space to manoeuvre when the car behind gave a blare of warning on his hooter. It was then that the traffic ahead started moving with more intent. 'At last!'

Lenny would have been relieved at that moment if it had not been for the low groaning noise he heard coming from the back seat. Another look into his mirror revealed a passenger frantically holding her tummy as she sat there with eyes clenched shut.

'Oh, gawd!'

Miraculously, a clear stretch of road ahead enabled Lenny to put his right foot down, perhaps a little harder than he should in a built-up area. Forty, forty-five, a little more. Was that beads of sweat he could feel on his forehead? He was able to pull out and overtake a car which was travelling just under the speed limit, then another. A London bus started pulling away from the curb ahead. Lenny's right foot went down harder as the groaning became louder behind him. He passed the bus with just a metre to spare. In his mirror he saw the bus headlight flash angrily, but it was the sight of his passenger's face that caused most concern, for it was screwed up as her head was thrown back against the head-rest.

'Hold on, luv! Don't push yet! Won't be long now!'

'It's okay, driver. Just a big fart I had to let go.'

Suddenly, the flashing of the bus headlights was replaced by the flashing of a blue light on a motorcycle coming up rapidly behind him. Glancing down at his speedometer, Lenny knew that the police bike was not intending to pass him and shoot of ahead, like they usually do, oh no, not this time. The bike did indeed pass him, but the rider indicated with his gauntleted hand that he was to pull over.

'Do you know this is a thirty-mile-per-hour speed limit sir?' enquired the officer as he pulled off one gauntlet, then the other.

‘Yes, officer.’

‘And do you know how fast you were going as you beat-up that bus, sir?’ Before Lenny had time to answer the pointless question the air was suddenly filled with the loudest groan yet. Sticking his head through the open window the officer took one look into the back of the cab and exclaimed, ‘Bloody hell, follow me!’

Lenny had sometimes wondered what it would be like to be part of a police escort, for seemingly out of nowhere, a second police motor-cycle joined them as they hurtled through the London traffic. Houses, offices, and shop fronts became a blur as slow-moving traffic pulled over to allow them through. Meanwhile, Clare continued holding and massaging her tummy as the pains regularly came and passed.

The blue lights on the two motor cycles ahead continued flashing. The Queen sat back in the comfort of the saloon, pleased that the opening ceremony of the new maternity clinic had gone so well, that morning. She was, of course, used to this method of passing through cities and towns, although she suspected that the new chauffeur was a bit out of his depth with his new experience. At least the police riders know where they are going, she mused as she contemplated the burger she would soon be eating for lunch. Plenty of tomato ketchup she was thinking as she closed her eyes with the image of her treat filling her thoughts, causing her mouth to water with the prospect.

As per normal, Piccadilly Circus was a heaving mass of traffic with vehicles of every shape and size changing lanes and hooting at each other, just for the hell of it. As the Queen's cavalcade entered the fray from one street, the escorted taxi emerged from another. Two London buses manoeuvred across the traffic, as they do, and between them, managed to separate the leading police motor-cycles from both vehicles for a brief moment before order was once again restored, with one car heading for the palace and the other, toward the hospital.

'Hold on a little longer luv,' said Lenny over his shoulder. 'Nearly there. The police riders must know something I don't 'cos they're taking us a different way.'

Meanwhile, the other car screeched to a standstill at the front entrance to the hospital. The staff were ready, thanks to the police officer having radioed a massage ahead. Before the unwary Queen had had a chance to open her eyes the back door swung open before she was hauled out and immediately placed on a trolly which was instantly whisked through the entrance door and along the corridor to the delivery room.

'Aigh say!' protested the lady from beneath the blanket that covered her.

'It's okay, dear,' said the porter who was pushing her through various groups of people passing along the corridor. 'Soon 'ave you sorted, nothing to worry about.'

'Let me oorf, you silly person. What about my burger?'

'Burger? Is that what you call it? They'll soon 'ave it out and screaming its head off.' Right here we are.'

'Thank you, porter,' said a fully gowned oriental gentleman through his mask. Let's get her onto the bed with knickers off, I want to see what we've got.'

'Aigh say.' shouted the Queen. 'Nobody takes my knickers oorf. Do you know who I am?'

'You could be the queen herself, for all I know,' replied the doctor. 'But those knickers have to come off.'

Meanwhile, at the palace, Clare was the subject of curious looks as the taxi driver assisted her up the steps and into the grand entrance. 'I don't know why the police brought us here, but the lady has just informed me that her baby is coming.' Lenny informed the various flunkies standing watching this strange apparition that had just appeared. 'Get her to a bedroom, NOW!'

And so it was, that as they were about to be escorted past the Queen's bedroom, the baby refused to wait any longer and started his journey into the world. Baby Henry was born five minutes later in the comfort of the Queen's bed, successfully delivered by a grinning Lenny.

It was later that afternoon when Her Majesty, dignity restored and properly dressed, holding Henry in her arms, replied to Henry's father's request. 'Yes, I would love to be Henry's godmother. And I wonder if you might consider being our window cleaner. It would be a full-time job, as you can see, so it might be better if you all move into one of our staff quarters. I will be able to watch Henry growing up. Aigh say, would you like a burger?'

The End

The Street

The street and houses looked the same, but somehow different. Apart from anything else, there were vehicles of all kinds parked along the kerb on both sides of the road, leaving very few spaces. Martin remembered how infrequently anything other than the odd bicycle or horse-drawn cart would use the road, with very few cars parked along its length. He recalled the games which were invariably chalked on the road, such as the inevitable *Hopscotch* as well as *London to York* and *The Spiral.* Then, of course, there would be a chalked footy pitch where coats or jumpers would be laid on the road to simulate goalposts. He smiled as he recalled the annoyance and catcalls if a passing vehicle caused the games to have to stop, that is, unless it was an ice-cream van in which case there would be the pounding of feet to various front doors with pleas for pennies for ice-lollies or wafers. His smile broadened as he remembered the rag-and-bone man who came round with his cart once a week with his call *"Raggybones,"* at least that's what it sounded like. The thing that broadened his smile was the recollection of him and his best mate, William, placing a half-gnawed dog's bone on the cart and demanding,

"Thrupence mister!" His vocabulary had increased by a few choice words that day. *Kiss-chase* became one of his favourite games once he passed the age of thirteen, he recalled, especially when Jenny played. She was not a fast runner but he had always run slow enough to be sure she would catch him. What she lacked in speed she made up in those prolonged kisses. He remembered how, as he and Jenny had grown into adolescence, the chase had developed into something more. His first sweetheart, his first … Where were his friends now, he wondered, what were they doing with their lives?

Thoughts of distant friends faded as Martin reached the place opposite his childhood home where there once was a bomb-site, now a modern house which looked odd amongst the old terraced houses. Standing on the kerb in front of the odd house, he looked across the road to take in the site of number sixty-one which he could see in a gap between two parked cars. The original varnished door was gone, replaced by a white plastic one, plastic that extended to both front room and bedroom windows. No go-cart outside. No cricket stumps chalked onto the wall between door and window, which had usually been scrubbed off by his mum while 'doing the step.' No net curtains, just brown plastic slats, half closed. With hands in his coat pockets, he stood there remembering the broken window caused by a cricket ball which would surely have been a sixer on a proper field. His mates had all scarpered by the time his dad got to the front door and spotted him with bat in hand and a look of horror and fear on his face. Yea, he paid dearly for that one.

'Can I help you?'

'What?' It was a young lady, holding the handle of a pushchair, who was demanding his attention. 'Oh, I was just reminiscing. You see, I used to live here, in number sixty-one over there.' He indicated, with a nod of his head, the house opposite.

'Did you say, number sixty-one?' the young woman asked, as though she was surprised.

'That's right.' Martin replied. 'Course, it looked a lot different all those years ago.'

'So, when did you move out?' she enquired.

'Oh, about twenty-two years ago. I would have been about seventeen. My father dragged us all up north where he thought his prospects would be better in shipbuilding on the Clyde. He's gone now, as also is my mother, both taken by a flu epidemic, five or six years later. I'm on my own. Never married. Never met the right girl up there. At least, none who compared with the girl I had to leave behind all those years ago.' He kicked an empty cigarette packet which was lying on the pavement and watched it skid into the gutter. 'I take it you live in this street?' he asked the young woman who was now bending over peering into the pushchair.

'Just about to wake up, I'll have to feed him soon. In answer to your question, I've lived here all my life. I was brought up by my mother, a lone parent. Like you, she never married. She always said that there was only room for one man in her heart, my father.' As she spoke, she looked up into the man's brown eyes and saw sadness, uncertainty, and hesitation. 'I hope you don't mind my asking, but what brought you back here? To this street, I mean?'

'I've moved back into this town. Just by chance, my company has opened a branch here, and I was offered the management, it's all to do with computerised systems. All a bit boring I'm afraid. I jumped at it. I've been down here for a week now and I couldn't resist re-visiting my past. I suppose I'm a bit lonely and … well, you never know … there was always the possibility of … Oh I don't know.'

Both suddenly became aware of the beginning of a cry coming from the pushchair. ‘Okay little one, mummy knows what you want.’ the young woman said as she leaned over the pushchair while rocking the handle.

‘Before you go,’ said Martin, ‘I know it’s a bit of a long-shot, but you wouldn’t happen to know if there’s a neighbour living in the street, called Jennifer? She would be about my age.’

‘Yes, there is.’ She hesitated, searching his eyes which failed to conceal the kind and genuine nature of the man. ‘She’s my mother’ She hesitated for a moment before saying, ‘Dad .... this is your Grandson, his name is Martin, the same as yours. Why don’t you come and say hello to Mum?’

The End

The Gate Keeper

With care, Reg dismounted from his touring bicycle before leaning it against the side of the small hut. He had enjoyed the familiar ride from his home, a small village a little over six miles away. He knew every bend and slope along the infrequently used narrow road across the moor, and depending upon the direction and strength of the wind, the best choice of his five gears along the way. Cycling was his much-loved hobby, a hobby which, on his days off, would take him to far off places within or beyond the boundary of the moor, often covering well over a hundred miles. He preferred to do these trips alone, not wanting to be held back by any less-fit riders. If the truth be told, it was actually more because he preferred his own company. This was just one of the reasons he had taken on the job advertised by Network Rail in his local newspaper all those years ago. *Gate Keeper required. This is a responsible position requiring the successful applicant to be reliable and capable of working alone and unsupervised. Experience not required as training will be given. Applicants must be of sound mind and physically fit. Phone York 7394 ext:8.*

It had been in Reg's mind for some time to quit his rent-collection job which he had held for far too long. He had found it increasingly depressing, not to mention harrowing, trying to squeeze money from housewives who would invariably be struggling to keep their homes together as they tried to ensure their children had food on the table. It had been heart-breaking on several occasions when his failure to collect rent that was well overdue resulted in the inevitable call by the bailiffs. The British Rail advertisement had appeared to be the perfect answer for him, so-much-so that he had had no hesitation in hurrying to the telephone kiosk on his street corner where he had rummaged through his pockets for the required amount of coins before dialling the number.

That had been fifteen years ago. As far as he had been able to make out, he had been the only applicant. The job was his, it even came with a slight uplift in his weekly wage packets, also with a modest pension. He was to discover that the responsibility of a "Gate Keeper" was to manually open the railway gates on a busy line across the moors whenever an occasional road vehicle appeared on the lane which crossed the lines at that point. He was to work an eight-hour rotating shift, his favourite being the morning one starting at eight-o-clock.

Although there were small pedestrian gates the larger gates were normally closed to road traffic until such time as a vehicle appeared, this might happen no more than three time in a single morning shift. On arrival of the vehicle, which would invariably sound its hooter as it approached the gates if the driver happened to be a regular user, Reg would give a wave of acknowledgement to the driver before hand-cranking his telephone to call the signalman further along the line. He was not allowed to open the gates to road users until such time as the signalman gave him the *All clear.* It was only then that he was able to leave his little hut beside the track to unlock the gates before manually pushing them open. It was his habit to open the far gate before attending to the one immediately in front of the waiting vehicle as he didn't want an impatient driver inching forward until the crossing was clear. It was all a part of the training. With the vehicle safely over the tracks, Reg had to close the gates to any further road traffic and lock them in place before phoning the signalman again to inform him that the crossing was, once again, clear for trains to pass through.

'Morning Reg, enjoy the ride?' Reg smiled as he snapped the padlock on his bicycle before looking up to see Bert, knapsack slung over his shoulder, emerging from the hut.

'Yes, thanks. Not too much head-wind. Busy night?'

'Nothing. Spent nearly all night working on the rigging of my model of the *Victory.* I've left it on the top shelf, shouldn't be in your way. Right, I'll be off then, me old mate.' Peering up at the clear sky Bert continued, 'Looks like it's set to be fine. Think I'll get some shut-eye for a bit then see about servicing this old rust bucket.' He nodded in the direction of his black Ford Popular which was parked in a clearing alongside the hut. 'See you tomorrow morning Reg, enjoy your book.' Surprisingly the car started on the second turn of the key, thus enabling Bert to reverse onto the road before pulling away from the crossing with a wave of his arm from the open window.

Having retrieved his lunch box and two paperback novels from his saddlebag, Reg gave a final glance at the clear blue sky before stepping into the hut. He was pleased to observe that Bert, as expected, had swept, and tidied up the interior. He was unable to resist taking a look at the carefully crafted wooden model of HMS Victory which was still under construction. The detail was amazing and, as always, Reg admired the skill and patience of the retired Royal Navy Chief-Petty-Officer who had settled for a quiet life as a Gate Keeper on the railway. *It takes all sorts* mused Reg to himself.

A mug of tea was the first priority for Reg, no sugar and not too much milk. A glance through the window, which Reg noticed could do with a clean, assured him there were no vehicles waiting to be allowed through the gates. Not that he was expecting any. Sitting at the small wooden table and picking up his nearly completed novel Reg noticed the appearance of the brown liquid in his mug beginning to change. The mug had started to tremble very slightly. Reg looked up to the old clock which was hanging on the wall above the table. *Eight fourteen, on time, fast train to York* he thought with a satisfied nod.

Tea finished, mug washed and dried, window cleaned, the day for Reg was much like every other day that he spent in the hut with his novels. He was well content, and life was good. What more could he want? Well, there was one thing he would have liked half way into the morning routine. He would like to be able to dispel the uncomfortable feeling of being watched. It all began after the first hour. As he had turned another page of the action-packed novel, eager to discover whether the girl managed to find safety, he unconsciously glanced up at the window, and was startled by the image of a girl staring through the glass, resulting in him jumping from the chair which had been tilted on its back legs. Chair and novel skidded together across the floor. Tripping over the chair, Reg fell against the door which swung open under his weight. Managing to remain on his feet, Reg regained his balance before swinging around the corner of the hut to confront the girl.

There was no girl.

Reg had spent as much time as he was able searching for any sign of the girl, but to no avail. There was nothing to indicate there had ever been a girl standing by the window. Company rules firmly stated that, apart from normal calls of nature (for which a small outhouse was provided) the duty Gate Keeper was to always remain in the immediate vicinity of the hut. As much as Reg would have liked to walk to the top of the slope overlooking the crossing to see if he could spot anything that would explain the sudden appearance, he was reluctant to break the rules.

The remainder of the day gave Reg time to ponder the strange occurrence, and throughout that day the uncomfortable feeling of being watched remained with him, so-much-so that he was unable to concentrate on his otherwise thrilling novel. It was with relief when the time came to hand over to Simon who had the evening shift. Convinced that it had all been in his imagination, perhaps brought on by the thriller he had been reading, Reg mentioned the one coal-lorry that had passed through, but nothing about the possible vision of the girl, when Simon asked the habitual question which was no longer funny, 'Busy, or really busy?'

The following day brought a silently drifting mist, not at all unusual on this moor. However, what *was* a little unusual was the fact that the mist lingered, even after the sun would be expected to burn it away. Convinced that the previous day's incident was all in his overactive imagination, Reg thought no more of it, that is, until the sound of rumbling wheels became apparent during the morning. Looking through the swirling mist beyond the glass, he was surprised to make out a horse and cart pulled up in front of the far gate. Surprised, because (i) he thought he knew all the local farmers who were likely to use the crossing, (ii) none ever used a horse and cart, and (iii) the man on the cart just sat staring through the mist at the railway gate without looking at the Keeper's hut. Even the horse was unmoving, simply standing as still as a statue, not even a toss of the head as might be expected. For fully a minute Reg stood and waited for any sign of impatience or expectation from man, or horse ... Nothing.

Not liking the uncanny feeling of unreality, Reg gave a shrug and cranked the handle of his telephone.

'Morning,' responded the signalman who Reg immediately identified as Clive, an old timer who had spent his entire working life on the railway. 'A bit spooky up there on the moor in this stuff, I imagine?'

'Yea, 'tis a bit. I've got a horse and cart here, never seen it before, how's the line?'

'A horse and cart? A bit unusual, isn't it? Have to wait a bit, goods train due there in seven minutes. Can't risk it, especially with a slow one like a horse and cart. You're clear to open up after it's passed you, won't be anything for another half hour after that. Call again once you've re-opened to the line. A horse and cart in this mist? Blimey.' The telephone receiver clicked in Reg's ear. The call was ended. Replacing the receiver on its cradle, Reg opened the door and slipped out into the damp mist to wave an acknowledgement to the cart driver while holding up his other hand, first with fingers and thumb spread, then with just three fingers, in order to indicate *a wait of eight minutes.*

No response ... Nothing. Both driver and horse just continued staring at the gate, neither of them moving in the drifting mist. With a shudder, whether from the cold dampness that clung to his jacket, or ... something else, Reg drew back into the relative warmth of the hut where he stood at the window, watching for any sign of movement beyond the far gate ... nothing. Normally, with such a wait, Reg would step out to greet and exchange a few words with the waiting driver. Not today though. It was frankly all too weird.

As his focus continually flitted from the unmoving apparition just beyond the far gate to the slowly moving second hand on the clock, Reg willed the approaching goods train to appear down the track. *How could eight minutes be so long?* He asked himself, more than once. He was not generally a superstitious man, or given to an irrational fear of the unknown, but something about this day, and the previous one, was lifting hairs at the back of his neck. Another glance at the clock to reassure himself that the second hand was still following its designated path around the clockface. *Come on, come on!* Reg muttered under his breath. Not wanting to look through the window but not being able to resist, his stare revealed nothing but a bank of mist. For a full circle of the clock's second-hand Reg stared through the glass. Slowly the mist thinned, enough to see the wet grass outside the hut, then the cinder path, then the nearside gate just a few yards away, then the far-side gate, then … nothing.

Must be going mad! What's wrong with me? Why am I seeing things that aren't there? Reg continued staring at the spot where the horse and cart had waited, that is until the quietness was disturbed by the sound of an approaching steam locomotive's whistle, followed by the roar of pistons, steel on steel, and the clanking of trucks passing over joints in the rail. As the brake-van swept passed his window, Reg's eyes were drawn to the empty road just before the mist enveloped the spot where the horse and cart had stood just a few minutes ago.

With trembling hands Reg lifted the telephone receiver to his ear while cranking the handle. 'Hello Reg,' It was something of a relief to hear Clive's steady voice at the other end. 'Your horse and cart's safely over then?'

'As a matter of fact, Clive,' breathed Reg, 'it must have turned around without me seeing it in the mist. It's gone now.'

'Strange,' responded Clive thoughtfully. 'Are you okay, Reg?'

'Why do you ask? I'm okay,' replied Reg a little too quickly, 'but I'll be glad when this mist clears.'

'Oh, no reason. You sounded a bit ... confused, that's all.'

'Thanks for asking, but I'm fine.'

'You can expect the ten-fifteen on the upline in three minutes. I suggest you hold anything that appears until after its passed, including horses and the odd cow or goat, but ring me first,' he finished with a chuckle. 'Bye for now.' After he replaced the telephone receiver back on its cradle Reg applied a lit match to the gas ring, noticing the slight shaking of his hand as he did so. What he could do with now was a strong mug of tea.

That mug of tea was never to reach Reg's lips however. With the kettle singing on the gas ring, he could not resist another glance at the road on the other side of the crossing.

'*Oh my god! Nooo!*'

What Reg saw at that moment sent a chill to his rapidly beating heart. It was a young girl, possibly aged about seven or eight, dressed in a grey pinafore. She was standing *inside* the far gate and was stepping forward to cross the downline and then on to the upline upon which the ten-fifteen was now due. Frantically swinging open the door Reg ran down the cinder path in the hope of saving the girl, shouting *'STOP!!'* as he did so. It was at that moment there was a high-pitched shriek of the whistle just before the train swept through the crossing, pistons a blur of moving rods, steam streaming back over the cab, streaming passed too quickly for the eye to focus on any individual carriage. Reg slammed into the closed gate, heart thumping, breath rasping in his throat. Too late.

How can there be no body? Reg asked himself time after time that afternoon. Nothing! No blood, no mutilated remains of a little girl. Nothing at all. And yet ... she had clearly been on the line as the train had swept through. Reluctantly, Reg felt the need to confide in Clive. He realised it would be a risk, he could lose his job if it was thought that he was cracking up. With receiver to his ear, he cranked the handle and waited. Regardless of the chill brought on by the mist, he felt beads of sweat on his forehead.

'Hello Reg, got another one? Not a horse and cart I hope?' With difficulty, Reg relayed his story, starting with the appearance of the girl the day before. He was relieved when Clive listened without interruption, apart from to pull a few levers as and when necessary.

'What do you think, Clive? Am I going mad?' asked Reg when he had finished.

'No, you're not going mad, my friend. You may not believe what I'm about to tell you.' Reg listened intently as the older man relayed the story of a young girl who had apparently been killed while crossing the line over seventy years earlier. A time when there were no gates on the crossing. She had been running after her father, a local farmer, who had set out from home on his horse and cart not knowing that his wife was slowly sinking into a bog having tried to rescue one of her lambs. Hearing his daughter calling to him, the farmer had swung round on his seat, only to see the little girl fall beneath a train. When he eventually got the broken body back to the farm all he could see of his wife was her bonnet resting on the surface of the bog. An inquest into the deaths of both mother and daughter was the last that anyone ever saw of the farmer. He had simply vanished.

'That was years ago,' exclaimed Reg once Clive had finished the story. 'Why is this happening now?'

'I don't know, Reg,' replied an equally mystified Clive. 'To my knowledge nothing like this has ever happened before.' You sure you're alright? I can arrange for a relief if you want to call it a day.'

'No, I'm okay,' replied Reg. 'Just a bit shaken up. I'll be fine now. Thanks for telling me the story.'

'Okay, you take care, and be sure to let me know if anything else crops up. Bye for now.'

It was toward the end of his shift. Reg had not been able to concentrate on his book, or anything else for that matter. The mist had finally melted away. Unusually, his eyes kept returning to the road, looking in both directions, not being sure what he was waiting for. Then it became time to sweep the floor, rinse the mug and check that all was in order for Simon to take over at four-o-clock, the whole time continuing to watch the crossing. Just one more train expected before the end of his day. It was as he turned from the sink to check the crossing again that something outside caught his eye. Just beyond the far gate a child appeared. It was a girl dressed in leggings and a pink duffle-coat. She was riding a child's scooter and heading straight for the small pedestrian gate situated alongside the main gate, a gate that was seldom used as there were very few folks who passed that way on foot. It was then that he realised that the girl was unaware of any danger as she held her scooter in one hand and pulled the gate open with the other. Reg could already feel the vibration of the approaching train as he shot out into the weak sunlight, down the cinder path and through the small gate. Aware of the steam locomotive bearing down on him, Reg shot across the lines, grabbed the girl and scooter, and tumbled into the long grass avoiding being crushed by less than a second.

With the girl screaming and struggling in his arms Reg was relieved to see a woman running along the road.

'Beth! Are you alright? Oh Beth, you could have been killed!'

'Mummy!' screamed the distraught girl. '*I nearly got run over.'*

'I know, sweetheart, you should not have scooted so far ahead and out of my sight. I've told you this before. Come here.' Taking the girl into her arms, the woman looked up at Reg who had regained his feet, and said, 'How can I ever thank you? You saved my daughter's life. If you had not been watching, it doesn't bare thinking about. Thank you so much. We've only just arrived here. We have a VW Campervan which we've parked in that old derelict farm just up the road. A strange place. It somehow feels that a great sadness is hovering over it. It gives me the creeps. Anyhow, we're moving on tomorrow.'

'Hope your little girl gets over the shock,' replied Reg while dusting himself off. It was at that moment that he saw the girl in the grey pinafore dress standing some fifteen yards away. She was smiling at him and nodding. Then with a wave of her hand she faded away.

Reg continued working as a Gate Keeper until his retirement eleven years later. Throughout that time, he read fewer books while on duty. How could he when spending so much of his time watching the road and the crossing. He never saw the girl in the grey pinafore dress again, although he spent a lot of his free time over the years wandering amongst the crumbled buildings of the derelict farm just up the road.

The End

The Old Lamplighter

Slowly, the old man pulled on his cracked hobnailed boots, remembering as he tied the string that had served as laces for many months now, the day his childhood sweetheart had proudly presented them to him on his fiftieth birthday. Mary had been gone for, what was it now? Fourteen, fifteen years? Maybe more. She had been a good wife, worked hard all her life, cleaning wherever she could, mostly for the gentry. Never complaining. Never missed a day. Good health, or ill. Made no difference. A ready smile, a kind word, a listening ear. A hot meal always ready for when he returned home from the pit. He smiled as he remembered that first kiss, down in the orchard. They had been *courting* for the previous six months. She had enjoyed that kiss as much as he, that was until she suddenly remembered her mother warning her that one kiss leads to more, and kisses lead to unwanted babies. She need not have worried however, babies never came, not then, not at any time during their lives together. Wanted, but not to be. He frowned as he tied the knot in the string of his second boot. She would have been a wonderful mother. He could still picture her face whenever a child came near while out walking. A look that spoke volumes, often ending with a tear in the corner of her eye, a tear which would be quickly swiped away with the sleeve of her coat. Not for them, sleepless nights, sticky hugs, broken toys, laughter, tears, stories by the fireside, skipping ropes and spinning tops. Still, they had been content. They had each other. The comfortable companionship born of love, trust, shared concerns, problems overcome, contentment. They had talked together, laughed together, cried together, and relaxed in silence together.

Boots securely tied, the old man stepped from the stool upon which he had been seated, and reached for his worn-out overcoat which, now lacking buttons, was also tied about his middle with string, well perhaps not string, more cord than string. Cap next, then the old woollen mittens which had been knitted by Mary those three weeks before she finally slept. Such a gift! He preferred not to use them too often, but when the winter frosts bit at the tips of his now crooked and stiff fingers, it's what she would have insisted upon. He glanced out of his scullery window, the view nothing but a brick wall just six feet away from the dusty glass. He had no need for the clock which was pawned too long ago to remember, the approaching evening light told him all he needed to know. It was time.

The quarter-full can of oil clonked onto the privy floor as he placed it down, having filled the metal cylinder at the tip of his pole. He carefully trimmed the wick, cursing under his breath at the uncontrollable shaking of his hands. *When did that start happening,* he asked himself? The light was fading fast as he closed the privy door and shoved the broken wall-brick against it with the toe of his boot. *Why does the darkness come faster than it used to?* The question he had been asking himself for several weeks now. *Must get a move on, or I'll be late.*

Giving the back door a final rattle to be sure it was closed, the old man shuffled down the alley between his end-of-terrace house and the neighbouring ball-bearing factory, to emerge onto the street, the first of two streets on his round. It was upon reaching the first gas lamppost in that street that he took out the box of matches from his coat pocket and, having extracted one of the matches, proceeded to scrape the sulphur against the side of the box. His wrinkled face briefly lit up in the gathering gloom as the match flared with a hissss. He applied the burning matchstick to the wick on the end of his pole before re-pocketing the box.

'Hello Mr Lamplighter.'

The old man swung round to see a young boy, probably no more than six years old, peering up at him. 'Why if it isn't young Charlie. Hello young man, what you up to then?'

'Nuffink. Just come to watch ya'

'Have you now? And what else may I ask?'

The boy, with a mop of un-combed hair, hands in the pockets of his grubby short trousers which failed to cover his scraped knees, hesitated before tentatively asking, 'Got any toffees today?'

'Toffees!' repeated the old man. 'Now let me see,' Dipping his free hand into the other coat pocket he made a great show of searching for something before ... 'Ah! What's this? Well bless my soul.' He slowly extracted his hand and examined the object which he had fished out. 'I do believe this might be a toffee,' he exclaimed. 'Now, how did that get in there, I wonder?' Still holding on to his pole, the old man crouched down and ruffled the boy's hair while handing over the much-appreciated toffee.

'Thanks Mr Lamplighter,' said the boy as he quickly unwrapped the sticky treasure. 'It's a nutty one. My favourite.'

'Your favourite, you say!' said the old man in amazement. 'Why, yesterday you said treacle was your favourite.'

'It was my favourite then, but now it's nutty ones. See you later.'

'Not for much longer,' the old man muttered to the boy's retreating back.

Reaching the pole up to the business end of the gas-light the old man hooked onto the brass chain which was suspended beneath the mantle, gave it a slight tug, which opened the gas valve, then moved the burning wick to the mantle. A dim light invaded the surrounding darkness as the old man painfully hobbled on to the next lamppost.

'Good evening, Mr Lamplighter.'

'Good evening, Mrs Lambert. Did you enjoy the potatoes and carrots I gave you yesterday, all fresh from my humble little garden?'

'I can't thank you enough, that's no lie. The kiddies were starving since I've not been able to afford to buy food for well over a week now. I was able to make soup with what you gave me, and I've got some left for tonight. Me leg's a bit better now, so I can go out and earn again in a few days. You're a good man and I'll not forget what you did, an' that's a fact.' The middle-aged lady withdrew into her passage with a smile before closing the door.

With the second lamp adding more light to the street, the old man slowly moved on until he drew abreast of No.14. Here, he lightly tapped on the door and waited. Eventually, a shadow briefly appeared at the window, followed by the rattling of a chain at the front door before it creaked open. 'Hello Nancy,' the old man said gently to the timid eight-year-old girl who stood looking up at him. 'How's Daddy today?'

'He's still not very well and has to stay in bed, but he's really happy about the books you brought round. He say's I'm to thank you for your kindness and that he will return them when he's better. I like the one about the big white whale, he's been reading it to me.'

'Well, that's good. Here, I have a toffee for you. Must go, or people will be bumping into each other in the dark. Good night, Nancy.'

‘Good night, Mr Lamplighter,’ replied the girl as she pulled the creaking door closed.

With the first street illuminated with the soft light that followed the old man’s progress his thoughts turned to the advent of electricity and all the changes it would entail, good or bad. Peering down the length of his second street he still could not get used to seeing the harsh light which very nearly defeated the darkness at the far end of the street. He noticed that several more of his old gas lamps had been replaced with electric lamps during that day, leaving only six old lamps for him to light. The whole atmosphere of the street was changed No longer homey, but seemingly cold and impersonal. He shook his head and muttered, ‘Progress! At least I won’t be around when the whole town’s all done, thank goodness.’

He had reached the third of the six lamps which were still left for his attention when a man with hunched shoulders, cap on his head, and both hands in his pockets, approached from one of the houses across the street. ‘Evening, Mr Lamplighter,’ he said with a grin. ‘Just three more to do, I see. When you’ve done, can you come over to our house, I’ve another favour to ask you. Seems

I'm often in your debt over something or other, just like most folk around here. If that's convenient, see you in half an hour?'

That's okay Albert. No problem, if I can help, all to the better. I'll be along as soon as the last one's done.'

With the last lamp lit and glowing as it should, the old man carefully smothered his wick, taking care not to spoil it, then retraced his steps to Albert's house, all the while wondering how he might help that jovial man. Last time, it was by fixing a broken gate, as working with timber was something he was good at. He used to be responsible for anything involving timber before he retired from the pit. On arrival at the house, he was surprised to see the front door partly open. *'Hello?'* he called. No answer. Pushing the door further open, he called louder, *'Albert? Are you there?'* Still no answer.

'Strange?' he muttered, then out of the darkness down the passage Albert's voice replied, *'Come on through, mate, mind the step.'* Feeling his way forward, the old man shuffled along the length of the dark passage, worried that he might trip over a bicycle, a discarded toy, a pram, or something.

'We're in here, mate,' came Alberts voice from behind the partly closed parlour door. 'Come on in.' Pushing the door open, the old man suddenly became aware of dozens of people crammed into the relatively small space, each suddenly lighting candles before the gas globes were lit by Albert. It was Albert who started the singing of *'For he's a jolly good fellow,'* quickly joined by all the others. It was then that he spotted the table crammed with food, lemonade, and beer. He also spotted Mrs Lambert and her children, Charlie and his parents, Nancy, and her father, now well enough to be out of bed it seemed, as well as so many folks whom he had helped in some small way over the years.

Thrusting a pint of beer into the old man's hand, Albert said, 'Electricity may have come to our streets, mate, but our hearts will always be lit by our dear old lamplighter. By the way, are you free tomorrow? Got a little favour to ask. Bring your saw.'

The End

Ink Isle

'Ink Isle. Strange name. Never heard of it before. Are you sure you've got the right one?'

'Course, I'm sure.' Terri answered indignantly. 'It's here in my diary. Head Office phoned it through to me last night while I was at a night club. "M" said it's almost as far north as you can get in Scotland and that it's to be treated as urgent as they want it done before the end of the year. Stop worrying, Ant, as long as you've got all the gear you need that's all that concerns you. I'll handle the rest of it.'

'Okay, everything I need is in the boot. Can't wait to see their faces as I shoot them. Pow! Done!'

Terri and Ant were a new team. This was to be their first mission, a mission none of the other teams were available to take on, according to "M". Early that morning, following a sleepless night, a messenger had delivered the package to Terri's apartment, and just a few minutes later Ant had arrived with the car. She was a little apprehensive if she were being honest with herself, but after all those weeks of training, what could go wrong? Identify the street, knock on the door, shoot, done. Simple. *Shame it had to be so far out. There must be a boat we can catch to get to the island,* Terri mused. A jumble of thoughts where tumbling through her mind as Terri watched the passing scenery. She had always wanted to travel, explore new places, meet interesting people. The Ad' had mentioned all those things. It was quickly established that she was *"The right sort"* so the job was hers. Last night was a bit of a celebration following the completion of her training. She had had no idea that things would take off so suddenly and unexpectedly, otherwise she would have been restrained with how much she was drinking.

Anthony was also new to the game. They had met for the first time that morning. Kind of good looking but a bit rough around the edges. Says he's been in the business for a few years but not with this outfit. Fancies something different for a while, more "face-to-face" as he put it.

'Oh, oh!' exclaimed Ant, breaking into Terri's thoughts as he also applied his right foot to the brake pedal while pulling into the side of the road.

'Something wrong?' asked Terri in alarm.

'Puncture!'

'Hell's teeth. Can you fix it?'

'Have to clear the boot of everything to get to the spare.'

Looking at her watch, Terri tutted and said, 'We still have at least two hours to go before we reach the harbour according to my map, and I'm hungry. We'll need to stop somewhere for food soon. So, let's get a move on. I'll help to unload.'

With the boot lid raised, Terri reached for the holdall which was closest to her when her arm was grabbed by Ant. 'Not that one. Nobody touches that but me.'

'Suit yourself,' replied Terri, shifting to one side to allow her partner to get to his precious gear.

It was just under an hour before they were back on the road. 'I can't believe you've never checked the tyre pressure of your spare,' complained Terri. 'My leg is going into spasms after all that pumping with the foot-thingy. I bet James Bond never had to do that with his Aston Martin.'

'What you complaining about? I bought you a burger at that service station, didn't I?'

‘Oh, you mean that stale bun with a bit of leather stuffed into it, do you? You didn’t even think to slosh some ketchup into it.’

‘Well, if you hadn’t spent so much time mending your face in the Ladies you could have got your own food.’

‘How gallant,’ retorted Terri. ‘Double O Seven always gets the romantic ones, however dangerous they are. What do I get? A grumpy mean old *“Nobody touches that but me”* bloke with more than one flat tyre to his name.’

‘Yea, but I can turn on the irresistible smile when needs be.’

‘Save that for the folk who are about to have their day changed,’ sighed Terri as she studied the brief.

Three hours later, standing on a pebbled beach covered in discarded plastic bottles, a variety of seaweed and a few other items best not to be thought about, the team of two stood gazing at the small island half a mile across the grey water. Terri was scratching her head as Ant hoisted his precious bag further up his sloping shoulder.

‘You sure you’ve got the right place?’ asked Ant.

‘Ink Isle, that’s it. That’s what it says on the ferry notice board, so yes, I am sure.’

'It also says the next ferry is tomorrow morning, or perhaps you didn't see that?'

'Yes, I did. But I also saw the small rowing boat tied to the pontoon. It even has those oar things in it. You can row us across,' replied Terri with an encouraging look.

'No, sweetheart, not in my contract. I do the shooting, that's it.'

Half-an-hour later, a small rowing boat is slowly approaching Ink Isle. Sitting on the transom seat is a sour-faced man nursing a holdall close to his chest. On the centre bench is an exhausted young lady who is, somewhat less than skilfully, repeatedly dipping the oars into the water. She is muttering 'James Bond gets to ride in a powerful motorboat with a passenger making sexy eyes at him, I have to make do with this leaking old pile of rotten wood with a smart-arse smirking at me.'

With the boat tied to a sewer outfall and the long muddy trek across the fields behind them, the couple arrive at the one and only occupied cottage on the island.

With the sun now well below the horizon and with winged bats flitting overhead in the gloom, the tired team walk quietly to the front door. A light can be seen through the curtains. A shadow moves across the room. An owl releases its mournful call in the coming night. The leaves above them rustle in the breeze.

'Okay, Ant,' whispers Terri nervously. *'This is it. Get ready to shoot.'* Satisfied that her partner is poised, she reaches for the door knocker only to see it move suddenly away from her as the oak door unexpectedly swings inward with a very loud creak. *Click ... Flash!* The darkness is shattered by the sudden burst of light as a highly fired-up Ant presses the trigger.

'What the ...!' The three of them stand transfixed on the threshold. *'Who are ye, and what you doing here at this time of night with that camera?'* demands an angry man. 'All visitors to the nature reserve should have left on the last ferry over an hour ago. You'll disturb the birds.'

'Congratulations!' yells Terri. 'You've won top prize on the Postcode Lottery.'

'What? Never heard of it. I don't do any lotteries. What ye blithering about?'

'Here, I'll show you,' returned Terri. 'Ink Isle, a bit smudged but this is your lucky day.'

'Let me see that,' demands the man while holding out his hand.

Terri triumphantly hands over the brief with her best well-rehearsed smile. Ant is ready with the camera and takes another shot of the frowning man.

'Put that ruddy camera away before you scare the birds even more, young man,' demands the man as he holds the forms and the cheque to the light from his hallway. 'This says IN8 1SL, not Ink Isle, you blithering fools. I believe you'll find you should be somewhere near Inverness, not here. Now, please leave this island quietly. I don't know how ye got here and I don't much care. Just go, and take that dumfounded camera with you. Postcode Lottery, whatever next?'

The End

The Autumn Years

Early morning frost which is yet to be claimed by the suggestion of warmth, clings to the swaying grasses.

Rustic gate posts gleam with glittering purity, made more so by its transience.

Ivy covered tree stumps, remnants of what had once been proudly swaying trees, gleam in the morning air, mantled by frost which is soon to be reduced to moisture that will cling throughout the coming day.

Long gone are the days of carefree meandering in the balmy airs of evening twilight.

The old man sits on the side of his unmade bed. Fading memories of golden years his remaining treasures.

Recollections, once so vivid, now reduced to fleeting pictures of unconcerned youth. Where did the time go? What trickery stole away the years of love and companionship?

Where are the children who once played at his feet? Gone are the colourful buckets and spades, used in earnest to hold back the incoming tide. A brief recollection of teenagers whose faces bore the same features as those carefree children. Shrieking laughter replaced by grunts and scowls.

Where swaying green leaves used to fill the air with their whispering and rustling, a lone robin quietly tweets his territorial presence on a naked branch, now exposed to the unseeing gaze of a hungry fox.

A flight of honking geese, in perfect vee formation, passes overhead. Where bound? Somewhere warm one might assume.

Ah, warmth. Warmth in the open air is nought but a memory now, pleasantly touching the politely clapping picnic parties following the sound of leather upon willow.

The old man sighs as he glances up at the locked window of his small apartment. It's been many years since he watched smoke tumbling from the tall chimney into the frosty air above the thatch cottage which witnessed his first breath. He can still recall the home-made rug on the cobbled floor before the blackened range, where multi-coloured rag became imaginary waves as he toyed with the crude wooden boat carefully crafted by his father.

A beautifully spun web, spanning a gap in the heather, trembles in the slight breeze, invisible yesterday, but now advertised by its hoary coating.

Hedgerows with the greens, reds, yellows and blues of those summery days, now bare, exposing bird-nests long since abandoned by fledglings when they set out on fluttering wings to the precarious lives ordained for them. Beneath, rabbit holes, also long abandoned by their furry creators. Where are those creatures now? Will they survive to be blessed with the return of warmth and abundance?

Life in whatever form it takes, is a precious gift. From early spring when hope and wonder transcends the gloom and hardship of winter, leading to the lengthening days of promise and rebirth, new beginnings, new friendships, new awakenings.

As a daffodil's petals blossom from buds to golden crowns, so the buds of early romance send their unmistakable fragrance into the air.

The old man wipes his moistened eyes with the back of his hand. A hand now bent with arthritis and scars of time. Blue veins criss-cross the skin, once tight but now loosely covering aching bones.

From those springlike days of blossoming romance, she was his life. His best friend, his soul-mate. She understood, forgave. She looked to him for comfort, support, guidance. She never doubted him, never faltered, never made demands. As she took her last few breaths on that cold November day, she looked up into has eyes and simply said, 'It was good, wasn't it? Thank you.' Then she was gone.

How many years have passed since that day? He doesn't remember. No matter. She lives on in his heart. Her memory will nurture him a little longer through the coming days of winter. The warmth of her love will sustain him, until?

With creaking bones, the old man carefully rises to his slippered feet and steps over to the window. He stares out into the garden. The pond is draped in ice. All is still. Nothing stirs. The trees in their unashamed nakedness are waiting. Waiting for what? Are they waiting for the same thing as he? He doesn't know, he cannot tell, for he no longer knows what he's waiting for. The words repeat themselves over and over in his head, 'It *was* good, wasn't it?'

Yes, it was good. But now autumn has claimed its rightful place. The waiting trees will one day mantle themselves with splendour. The geese will return. The hedgerows will once again provide shelter. The old man knows he won't see any of this. It *was* good, and will be so, again, when he is reunited with his lost love in a new spring. A new beginning.

The End

Mighty Lady

Silently, the twelve-year old girl stands on an empty wooden pallet surveying her surroundings. It has been a long journey for her, firstly hitching a ride to the train station on the local farmer's milk cart, then the long wait until the early morning milk train puffed into the station in a cloud of steam and a shower of soot. It hadn't been too difficult for her to lug her cardboard suitcase through the open carriage door, since it contained few possessions beyond a change of underclothes and a slightly newer pinafore dress than the one, she is currently wearing.

Her father had been poorly with Tuberculosis for as long as she could remember, and on the day before he finally took his last strained breath, he had handed May an envelope with his whispered instruction that she should open it after his burial. This she did after the few neighbours who had turned up, more out of curiosity than genuine concern, had left the rented cottage, having greedily helped themselves to most of the jam sandwiches which May had prepared earlier.

The untidy scrawl on the parchment contained within the envelope was brief. May was literate enough to decipher the words set down by her father. *"Leave the cottage, catch a train to Southampton. Money in my best going-out shoes. Look for your Uncle Silas on his tugboat. He will take care of you. Love, Pa."*

May had never been to Southampton or even seen the sea, having lived in the small iron foundry hamlet in Asfordby Valley throughout her young life. How she was to find this Uncle Silas and his tugboat once she had arrived in Southampton, she had no idea.

Now, with the help of a kind gentleman at the railway station, she had found her way to the port where she had carefully stepped over railway lines or around oily puddles, also, stacks of crates and wooden barrels of something or other. She was amazed at the bustle of activity going on around her, cranes lifting heavy loads from steam-ships tied to the quay, men with loaded barrows narrowly avoiding her as they scurried away, railway trucks being shunted in every direction. She was fascinated, but no more so than what she is now looking at from the advantage of the pallet. On the stretch of water in front of her, there are steam-ships in every direction. Some tied to the quay with cranes lifting cargo out or into them, others slowly moving through the water, either arriving or leaving the busy port. Some are being towed or pushed by smaller boats, each of which has a tall funnel belching out black smoke. Many are tooting their hooters, almost as though they are talking to each other. She has read enough when attending school, to realise that these boats are known as tugs. Therefore, perhaps it's one of these that's owned by Uncle Silas. But which one?

May steps down from the pallet and walks over to an empty barrow, upon which she places her suitcase. She is hungry after the long journey without having eaten. She remembers the left-over jam sandwich she had packed in her case early that morning. Untying the cord which is securing the suitcase lid, for the catches are no longer working, May rummages through her few possessions until she finds the sandwich which is wrapped in an old tea-towel. She unwraps the food and places it on the bed of the barrow before retying the cord. Suddenly there is a white flash and flutter of wings as a scavenging seagull appears from nowhere, picks up the sandwich, and flies off. Before May has time to react, her sandwich is gone. Her eyes follow the bird, only to see her meagre meal drop from its cruel beak into the oily water beneath.

'You must be new around here.'

Startled, May turns around to find that she's looking at a boy of around her own age, maybe a little older. With hands deep in the pockets of his rather dirty trousers the boy is grinning at her beneath a mop of ginger hair.

'Pardon?' May has no idea what to say beyond that one word, for she had clearly heard what the boy had said.

'Only an incomer w'd leave food unguarded in these docks. What ya doing 'ere? Missed yer boat or somat?'

Feeling embarrassed at her stupidity, and at the same time, angry with the grinning boy, she retorts, 'As a matter of fact, I'm looking for my uncle, not that it's any of your business.'

To her surprise, the boy bursts into laughter before gathering himself and saying, 'Uncle, is it? Do you know which one? I've got loads of 'em callin' round to our 'ouse. It all depends on which ship's in. Got a name?'

'May,' replies the flustered girl, for she can guess what the pertinent boy is talking about.

'Na, not *your* name, I meant what's the name of this uncle, your lookin' for? Ya never know, I might know 'im if 'e works the docks. Course, if he's a sailor, no chance.'

'Silas. He's my Uncle Silas,' says May after a slight hesitation. 'He's the owner of a tugboat, but I don't know which one.' As she says this, May is looking back at the water where she can see at least three such boats gathered around a cargo ship which is coming up the stretch of water toward the dock. There are two other tugs stationery in the water, as though waiting for the ship.

'Silas? Really?' says the boy while running a grubby hand through his mop of hair. 'Well knock me down if I'm not the son of a whore. Silas is the name of my skipper. Cap'n Silas Fletcher.'

For the first time this day, May is smiling. 'That's *my* name, I am May Hope Fletcher. Your captain must be my uncle.'

'Could be, though 'e's never mentioned 'avin' no niece.' Adjusting the canvas bag held over his shoulder the boy says, 'Come on, I'll take you to 'im. My name's Jimmy by the way, better known as "Fingers".

Not entirely sure she can trust this boy, especially with a name like that, May picks up her re-tied suitcase and follows him along the quay. They pass various ships, including a rather grand ocean liner which has ribbons stretched between waving passengers on the deck above and folk looking up from the quay while waving back.

'Just about to leave for Australia,' says Jimmy who has stopped to allow May to catch up. 'I'm gonna be on one of them ships one day when I'm older. I'll be workin' in the engine room, you'll see.'

'Do you know about engines?' enquires May who is thrilled by the sight of all those colourful ribbons connecting the liner to the shore, never having seen anything so gay.

'Do I know anything about engines! Who do you thing keeps the engines workin' on yer uncle's old rust-bucket?'

'Why do you call it that?' enquires May.

'What, "rust-bucket?" You'll see,' replies the grinning boy. 'Come on, not far now.'

'Where's that damn boy got to?' mutters the bearded man to himself as he looks along the quay from the modest height of his bridge wing. 'Can't hang around tied up here all day while he swans off looking for a few nuts and bolts. I've a mind to tan his hide when he shows up.' Tutting to himself, the skipper of *Mighty Lady* steps back into the bridge house. He is wearing an old uniform jacket, which has seen better days, beneath a peaked cap with a white cover, at least it was white many years ago, but is now various shades of grey. Silas removes his pocket watch, glances at its dial, sighs, then picks up his mug of tepid coffee which he gulps down in one swallow. He now accepts that he will not be working his tug anymore this day. He steps over to the brass engine room telegraph lever alongside the large wooden wheel, then hesitates before moving the lever to "Finished With Engines". He waits for the repeat signal from the engine room before leaning into the voice pipe and saying, 'Okay

Sandy, we'll pack it in for the day. Still no sign of Fingers, I've no doubt he'll find the parts you need. You can finish the repairs in the morning. You just need to keep the old girl running for another two weeks, then she's off to the breaker's yard. I'll see about cooking something up for our supper. Won't be much though. You can blame that blasted cook for deserting us last week.'

Silas takes a last look around his bridge before going below. He prides himself on the tidy and clean state in which he has always maintained the wheelhouse, although the outside of the craft, now approaching the end of its busy life, is looking in bad shape now. She is covered in rust. Painting the hull and working gear has become a constant battle and a pointless waste of time. The woodwork is peeling and the brasses are now permanently dull. Silas will be taking on a newly built, and more modern tug after a short period of leave at the end of the month. He is still not overly happy about leaving *Mighty Lady* to her fate, for she has served him well since he first stepped board as Second Mate, some twelve years ago and before working hard enough to eventually become Skipper.

Removing a soft cloth from the screen ledge, Silas dusts the engine telegraph lever, the wheel, and the compass housing, before stepping out onto the bridge wing where he will descend the steel ladder to the lower deck. As he does so, he spots Fingers ambling along the quay as though he's out for a stroll. Even worse, he's talking to a girl, a girl carrying a battered suitcase.

Cupping his hands, Silas shouts in the direction of the approaching lad, *'Boy! What do you think this is? An evening stroll in the park with a floosy you've just picked up? Get yourself aboard and down below, and you'd better have those spares you went for!'*

Grinning up at his captain, Jimmy says, 'I got someone 'ere wants to meet you.'

'What the hell you talking about, boy? I'm not interested in any female, especially those just out of the cradle. Get rid of her. Now!'

'You'll be interested in this one, skipper,' returns Jimmy. 'I'm bringing her on board.'

'The hell, you are. And how many times do you need to be told that you address me as "Captain" or "Sir". Saying this, Silas quickly descends the ladder to meet the boy as he steps from the gangplank. His anger increases as he sees the girl, hesitantly stepping from the quay onto the gangplank, clearly intending to follow the boy. *'Stay there, whoever you are,'* he shouts across the gap. *'You've no business aboard this boat.'* Turning and glaring at the still grinning boy and barely containing his anger, he says, *'Fingers, I told you to ger rid of her.'*

'Hello Uncle Silas.'

'What the!' Swinging around, Silas is confronted with the girl who is now standing on his stained deck.

'What did you call me?' he demands of the girl.

'Uncle Silas,' she pauses to let that sink in, then continues, 'I am May, your niece. Pleased to meet you, too.'

'May? ...You're May? Irene's girl?'

'That's right. My father is ... *was* Albert.'

Needing time to process this sudden revelation, Silas turns to Jimmy who is still standing there with that stupid grin all over his face. ‘Did you get those parts, Fingers?’

‘Yes, Skipper, all in my bag.’

‘Well don’t just stand there like a grinning monkey, take them down to Sandy, and I won’t even ask from where you got them.’

‘You owe Cap’n Fisher on *Prancing Lady* a favour or two.’ With that, the boy disappears through a bulkhead doorway.

Turning back to the girl who has not moved, Silas gruffly says, ‘You best come to my cabin, here give me that case. Follow me.’

Ten minutes later, Silas stares at the girl who he now accepts as family. She is seated on a stool in front of his small desk, hungrily biting into her third biscuit. ‘So, your mother died two years ago, and now you say my brother died last week. I am sorry for your loss my dear.’

'Thank you. You are my only family now. I can clean and polish and I'm a good cook. Can I stay here with you? I won't get in your way, you'll see, Uncle.'

'Yes, you can stay with me, but I have to be honest with you right from the start.' Silas hesitates to gather his thoughts. 'You see May, my dear, I may not be your uncle.'

'Oh,' is the only word May utters.

Leaving his captain's chair Silas steps around the desk, kneels in front of the girl and takes one of her hands in his own, before continuing. 'There is no easy way of saying this, May. So I'll come straight to the point. You see ... I may be your father.' May stares into Silas's crinkled eyes but says nothing. She waits for her ... "whatever" to continue. Silas clears his throat several times before continuing. 'You see, before you were born, Albert and I lodged with your mother for a bit. We had come to Asfordby looking for work in the foundry. We had been discharged from the cargo ship we had been working on together for several years. We thought we had seen enough of the sea and had decided to make a go of it, somewhere ashore. Your mother had a notice in the window saying that rooms were available. Well, the long and short of it is that we moved in on the same day that we were taken on in the foundry.' Silas paused long enough to get to his feet and step over to a small cupboard. 'I need a whisky,' he says. May notices the tremble in his hand as he pours a large tot before taking a gulp.

'Please go on?' she asks.

'You must understand, your mother was lonely following the death of her first husband. Well, not long after we had moved in, she and I ... did it. Two months later, she was pregnant with you. After getting over the shock a few days later, I decided to do the right thing and ask her to marry me. She turned me down.'

'Why?' asks May, not looking at all surprised.

'She apologised and said she was sorry and that she and Albert had also been ... well you know. She went on to say that she had no idea which one of us was the father, and that she had already accepted Alberts proposal. I stayed on till you were born and that's when we decided together that you should be called May because you *may* have been Albert's or you *may* have been mine. It was your mother who gave you your second name, "Hope", she never said why.'

Silas takes another sip of whisky before continuing, 'I felt like an intruder in your family after that, so decided to return to the sea, that's when I joined this tub. I never saw any of you after I left, till now.' Silas is finished. He sits down in his chair and studies May to gauge her reaction to his confession. He is a little puzzled to see that rather than being shocked, May is sitting quite calmly, thinking.

'Thank you for being so honest with me, Uncle … Father. Now I must be equally honest with you. You see, before mother died, she told me that I ought to know that just before you and my father, your brother, moved in, she had slept with another man who lodged with her for a few weeks, I can't remember his name. Anyway, she was not sure which one of the three of you was my true father. She said that she loved you two brothers equally and that it was her greatest *hope* that you would never find out about the other man during her lifetime. That's why she gave me my second name, "Hope".

'Oh, my dear child,' says Silas. 'It's all in the past now. You've been through so much. I want you to know, I *may* be your uncle but I *hope* I'm your father, for if you'll have me, that is what I intend to be.'

Smiling, May Hope Fletcher lifts herself from the stool, walks around the desk, plants a kiss on the captain's forehead and asks, 'Where's the kitchen, Father?'

The End

All In a Day's Work

VICTOR

The fiery red orb of the morning sun flitted through the leaves of a variety of trees which lined the avenue. Traffic was building into the start of rush hour, although it had become quieter since Victor had left the main road. Glancing over his shoulder, he steered his bicycle around a milk float while continuing to peddle hard. He knew he was going to arrive early, for that was his intention. He wanted to be at the gate in time to see his new workmates arrive, introduce himself and find out where he should park his bike. His heart was hammering in his chest, as much through nervousness as the effort he was putting into pumping the peddles.

Victor loved cycling, preferably on his own. He was not fast, more of a plodder, a speed more suitable for the long-distance rides he so much enjoyed during the weekends. This ride was different however. He was cycling to his first job, having left school the previous week after reaching his sixteenth birthday. It had originally been his intention to stay on at the Secondary

Modern school to take his GCE exams, but his mother wanted him out earning, so that was that. As he continued his journey, Victor reflected on how his mother had accompanied him to the Youth Employment Office and accepted this job in the corset factory on his behalf. She had even attended the interview with him, impressed with the three pounds, ten shillings he would be paid each Friday. 'You can keep a pound, I'll have the rest,' she had said on the bus after the interview with Mr Dines, the factory manager.

It would not be accurate to say that thc family was poor. It was simply that they were forced to live hand to mouth during this time of depression when every shilling counted. Now that he was employed, Victor was determined to save up for a new bike, one with at least ten gears, but for now, the one his dad had built up for him, using parts from his shed, would have to do.

His thoughts were suddenly interrupted as a black cat dashed from a garden gate, straight across the road in front of him. Swerving, he managed to miss the cat but unfortunately hit the curb, causing the bike to topple. This resulted in Victor skidding head-first along the pavement.

'Oh, my poor Tiddles,' wailed an elderly lady who had seen the whole incident from her front door through which the cat had slipped out while she was collecting her milk from the step. 'I hope you haven't harmed him with your reckless cycling. I've a good mind to report you to the police.'

'I missed the ruddy thing,' said Victor as he sat up and inspected his grazed elbows and knees. 'What about me? Look at what it's done to me! Can't you keep it under control?'

'It's your own fault,' replied the lady disdainfully. 'You're all the same, rushing about everywhere.' With a meaningful look, the lady hunched her shoulders and turned back to her garden gate while muttering something Victor preferred not to hear. Lifting his bike, Victor groaned as one glance told him that he would not be riding it any further that day. The front wheel was buckled and one of the peddles was bent.

'Blast! Now I will have to walk,' he muttered before picking up the damaged bicycle. Before setting off however, he opened the neck of his duffle-bag to be sure that his acceptance letter was still there. *Wouldn't want to lose that,* he thought to himself.

With several hundred yards to go, as Victor pushed the sorry looking bicycle along the pavement, he became aware of the sound of a siren coming from the direction of the factory gates. By the time he arrived at the entrance he saw the last few ladies disappearing through the front entrance to the building. He was alone in the car park.

Heck! Now what do I do? he thought to himself. Looking around the car park, he noticed a bicycle rack beneath some trees in the corner. Feeling conspicuously alone, he made his way in that direction, certain that many pairs of eyes were following his progress. With the bike parked, Victor adjusted his duffel-bag over his shoulder before limping across to the doorway where he had seen the ladies entering the building.

'Good morning, can I help you?' The question came from a young lady who was seated behind a desk in a lobby which was intended to be a reception. She was clearly a few years older than he; her head was covered in some sort of style he had seen on film stars on the telly, her hair was purple. She was peering up at him through the purple strands.

'My name's Victor Bunce, I'm new and I'm to report to Bob Callow,' replied Victor in a single breath.

With raised eyebrows, at least what Victor could see of them, the young lady leaned forward over a portable switchboard and pressed some tabs. There was a pause during which Victor cleared a throat which didn't need clearing, simply to break the silence, and studiously avoided eye contact with the young lady, as was his custom.

'Suddenly the embarrassing silence was broken as the young lady said, 'Bob, I've got a bloke here who says he's a new starter and is to report to you. Says his names Victor Bunce … that's right.' Victor became aware of her scrutiny. 'Yea, I know he's late. Looks like he's bin in a fight, or somat.' Another pause, then Miss Hair flicked some tabs before saying to Victor, 'He's sending someone over for you.' With that, she reached under the desk and produced a copy of "Woman's Weekly" which she started thumbing through. With no chairs available, Victor was forced to stand and wait. He avoided further eye contact with the young lady, preferring instead to gaze out into the car park as though something really interesting was happening out there.

'Hello, Victor Bunce?' It was a girl of about his own age who had suddenly appeared as if by magic.

'Yes,' was all Victor could think to reply.

'Follow me, please,' she said quietly. Without looking back at him, the girl, who was dressed in some kind of overall, swiftly led him away from reception, along a bare corridor, through a double-door and past a stone staircase from which Victor became aware of a loud humming noise.

'That's where the machinists work.' This was the first time the girl had spoken to Victor since leaving reception. 'The canteen's up there, you have to walk past all the girls for your lunch if you want something cooked,' she called back over her shoulder as she walked a few more paces to the end of the corridor and another set of double-doors. Pushing one of the doors open, she stepped aside to allow Victor to pass through. 'That's Bob's office, over there,' she said. At least, that's what Victor assumed she had said for his ears were suddenly full of noise.

This was a large room about the size of three tennis courts. It must have been at the end of the factory as there were windows along two of its walls. The room appeared to be arranged in two separate halves, one being lines of long benches with folds of material being laid out, while the other, on the window side, contained a number of machines in a long line. Victor's eyes swept around the busy room, taking in the men and women who were to be his workmates. All were industrially attending to whatever their work involved, although he noticed a few curious looks in his direction and a nudge or two, followed by a laughing comment.

Victor became aware that the girl was no longer with him, he had no idea where she had gone. Feeling overwhelmingly embarrassed, he followed a pathway between some of the benches, in the direction of the office the girl had previously pointed out. The grinning faces, as he passed the benches, became a blur. He was focussed on the open door of the office ahead of him. The twenty seconds it took to reach that door seemed more like twenty minutes to this boy who had been suddenly thrust into a strange and scary world of grown-up workers.

LINDA

As Linda arrived back at her bench, she resumed the laying out of patterns she had been doing before she had been sent to collect the boy.

'What's he like?'

'I don't know. He's tall and sort of quiet. A bit scruffy. He looks like he's been in some sort of accident. I felt sorry for him.' Linda was speaking to her best friend in the factory, a lady in her thirties who was married to one of the cutters. This couple had taken her under their wings when she has first arrived in the factory back in the winter. She had been appointed to Dorothy from the beginning, to be taught her job of laying-out. Apart from Dorothy and Mike she had yet to cultivate other friendships, being a rather shy and quiet young lady. Linda watched from beneath her eyebrows as Victor approached the foreman's office door.

<u>VICTOR</u>

Approaching the door with trepidation, Victor was very much aware of how late he was, as well as the state of his elbows and knees. Seeing the middle-aged man sitting behind his untidy desk reading something he had just removed from a file, Victor timidly knocked on the open door with his fisted knuckle. The foreman continued studying the paper he was holding until just before Victor was about to knock again, 'Well, don't just stand there, boy. Come in and kindly tell me the time.' Taken aback, Victor glanced around the office until his eyes rested on the clock which was obviously in clear view of the foreman.

'Um ... Half-past-nine?' he replied hesitantly, not sure if that was the information being requested.

'Half an hour past nine?' enquired the foreman while still apparently studying his piece of paper. Strange, I was given to understand that someone by the name of Victor Bunce was to report to me at nine. Is that you by any chance?'

'Yes, sir.'

Looking up for the first time, the foreman peered over his half-moon spectacles to study Victor from short-back-and-sides to his somewhat scruffy shoes, before asking, 'What happened?'

'Came off my bike, sir.'

'Okay, we can dispense with the "Sir", call me Bob. If you can't manage that, it's "Mr Callow". Are you in pain?'

'Pardon?'

'Have you hurt yourself, apart from what we can see?'

'Oh, no Sir ... Bob.'

'I am not Sir Bob. Not yet, anyway. Okay, perhaps you have a good excuse for arriving late, but do not make a habit of it if you want to work here. Follow me.'

Abruptly the foreman was out of his chair and walking through the still open door. Taken by surprise, Victor did his best to keep up as he limped along behind the foreman, between the benches, back into the corridor and up the stairs where the humming noise grew ever louder with each step upward. Guessing that he was soon to encounter hundreds of women working on their sewing machines, Victor was unprepared for what was to come. Passing through yet another set of double-doors, one of which was being held by the foreman, the humming noise became an insistent clattering, rather like a steam train passing through a station. Victor's eyes took in the endless rows of women of all ages beavering away on their machines. His cheeks burned as he noticed many suggestive looks and the winks of some of those nearest the walkway. Once again, he was following the foreman, feeling very much like a child following a teacher to the headmaster's office for some heinous crime like chewing gum in a maths lesson. Above the din, Victor was sure he could hear wolf-whistles coming from behind him. Rather like a football crowd the wolf-whistling was taken up by the whole assembly, becoming progressively louder until all the ladies had joined in, thus creating a noise that overtook the sound of a steam train passing through.

'Take no notice,' advised the foreman. 'They do that with all male starters. Okay, this is it, the first-aid room. We don't want you smearing blood over everything you touch, do we? When the nurse has finished with you, come back to my office.'

If asked for his opinion, Victor would say that he had not had a very auspicious start to his first hour of employment. With his injuries cleaned and dressed, the gauntlet of hobbling along the walkway amidst ribald comments from some of the women had to be faced. He arrived back at the foreman's office only to find it was unoccupied. Looking around the busy room, several ladies met his eyes and pointed over toward the corner of the room where he saw the foreman, standing alongside a large machine, about the size of a family car, beckoning him to come over. Passing between several of the long benches Victor was fascinated by the sight of cast-iron cradles moving along rails on the edge of the tables dispensing repeated layers of material as they moved backwards and forwards.

'Okay lad. Glad to see you looking more presentable. Starting tomorrow, this will be your machine. It's called a "Jigger" for reasons that will become apparent. It's big, it's powerful and it's dangerous. One lapse of concentration and it will eat your fingers, hand, or even arm.' Pointing to a man in his early twenties working the Jigger alongside, the foreman continued. 'That's Fred. You can spend the day with him while he introduces you to the Jigger and shows you how to operate it and do some cutting.' Victor glanced over to Fred who gave him a cheerful nod while crouching over his own machine. 'First though, I want you to fetch a bucket of soapy water from the caretaker's room, that's down the ramp over there, and then wash the blood off the table and blade of your Jigger.' It was only then that Victor saw the large stain on the tabletop alongside him. 'If you do well over the next few days, I will consider allowing you to become a trainee cutter, otherwise you'll have to be on pattern layout till we decide what to do with you. Understood?'

'Yes, sir … I mean, Bob.'

'Good lad.' Turning to Fred, he said, 'He's all yours after the tea-break, Fred. Look after him. He's going to clean his Jigger up till then.' Waiting for Bob to walk away, Fred left his machine and stepped over to where Victor was still gazing at the stain.

'I can't believe he's asked you to do that,' muttered Fred. 'I can only assume it's a kind of warning to you.'

'What happened?' asked Victor, already guessing most of the answer.

'Until Friday, this was Trevor's machine. He got careless and cut his thumb off. He won't be back. Funny, we never did find that thumb. You alright? You're looking a bit green.'

Having done his best to wash away the stain, Victor was relieved to hear a ringing bell which announced the fifteen-minute tea-break. Fred switched his Jigger off and beckoned Victor to follow him in the direction being taken by several others in the room. He noticed that others remained at their machines and benches and were pouring tea from thermos flasks which were retrieved from their bags. Victor picked up his duffle-bag and followed Fred down the ramp he had previously used to fetch the bucket of water. He soon found himself in a clear area in dispatch which contained a variety of tables and stools. 'This is where you come at lunchtime, unless you want something with three veg upstairs, although I wouldn't recommend it.' Addressing the room in general, Fred announced to the chattering group 'This is Victor. He's replacing Trevor.' Placing his arm around Victor's shoulder he pointed to several people, saying; 'That's Norman, he thinks he's an engine-driver, that's Barry he's talking to, he's still living the war as a flight engineer who imagines his Band-Knife is a Lancaster Bomber, that's Scabby over there, she's always picking scabs on her face and arms, as you can see. That's Huggy Hen over there, she loves big hugs if she can catch you. She says she misses her dogs during the day, so has to hug something else. Oh, and that tall chap over there with the stupid grin on his face is Tony.' Calling across the room to the man who was seating himself on a stool near the tea-urn, Fred asks, 'How's your Fudd, Tony?'

'Steaming,' came the reply.

'Turning back to Victor, Fred remarked, 'No idea what that means but that's how he likes us to greet him. Your locker's over there, by the way. You can park your stuff in there. It's called a

"Locker" but none of them lock, so I suggest you don't bring valuables in here. Sit down over there when you're ready, I'll get you a mug of tea. Milk and sugar?'

Seeing others lighting cigarettes, Victor, after checking his Acceptance Letter was safe, rummaged about in his duffle-bag before producing a pipe, a tin of tobacco, and a box of matches. Relieved that the pipe had suffered no damage from his accident, he opened the tin and started filling it with his aromatic tobacco.

'What's that?' It's Tony who had walked over to greet the lad.

'Oh, it's my pipe.'

'Blimey! We've never had a pipe-smoker in here before, apart from Sue, that is. She's gone now, died of throat cancer due to her habit. Been smoking it long?'

Not wanting to confess that he had bought the pipe on Saturday in order to be manly, Victor replied, 'A while, I like it more than cigarettes.' The truth was that he had made himself sick on one cigarette the previous week and that his attempts to smoke the pipe inevitably produced a hollow feeling in his stomach which he was hoping would be a temporary problem.

Victor was relieved when Fred returned with the tea and started a conversation with Tony about the match on Saturday. It was clear to Victor that these two were close friends, and hoped they would accept him also as a friend.

LINDA

Surreptitiously watching Victor follow Fred down the ramp, Linda wondered what it would be like to be able to talk to the new boy. *He looks so nervous and unsure of himself* she thought. *Quite good looking though. I wonder what it would be like to have a boyfriend?* Linda had no idea that Dorothy had noticed her faraway look.

VICTOR

Standing alongside Fred's jigger, Victor watched as his new friend seated himself in the recess at the front of the table. 'Right,' said Fred. 'As you know, this is called a "Jigger", we've got three of these, Norman's over there, this one, and yours. All the others are "Band Knives", more modern than these old Jiggers. With the Jigger the two-foot-long blade is held between two cast-iron arms, one beneath the table, the other, as you can see, is above the table. When you switch on, the arms jig up and down very fast and the blade does the same through the slit. On that trolly there, you can see layers of material about two inches thick with the top layer marked out with the patterns, all held together with clamps, like this, see?' Fred had pulled a block of pink elastic material toward him. Victor could see that on the top layer there were four different shaped patterns marked out. 'All we have to do,' continued Fred, 'is to pull the block through the knife, carefully following the pattern.'

'Isn't there a guard?' asked Victor.

'Should be. They've all been taken off as they get in the way. You just need to be careful,' grinned Fred. 'A word of warning before I switch on. As the blade speeds up, if you hear a loud bang, hit the deck like your life depends on it. It means the blade has snapped and it could fly off in any direction above or below the table. Best to be standing till the Jigger's going at full pelt, at which time you know it's all okay.'

'Blimey!' croaked Victor in alarm.

'Don't worry about it too much, it only happens about twice a year. Come to think of it, it has been about six months since old Norman's went. Poor old man messed his pants, they had to send him home because he stank too much. Where was I? Oh yes, another thing, you're responsible for keeping your blade sharp. Blunt blades can be dangerous as the material doesn't glide through and you have to pull harder. You'll feel when it needs sharpening. Then, you'll need to take it upstairs to Vernon; he's got the grinder. This one's about due, we can take it up there after lunch. Come to think of it, we'll take yours up at the same time. Now, watch as I switch on.' Fred got to his feet, swung the seat out of the way under the table, gripped a small lever on his right and pushed it forward, Slowly the cast-iron arm began to rise as the blade moved out of the slit. Faster, it descended, faster still, it climbed, then again, faster, until the movement was almost too fast to follow. The machine was running at full speed. As the table trembled beneath Victor's hands, he was mesmerised by the sight of the unguarded blade whipping up and down through the slit in the table. Fred slid a block of the pink material across his table onto the far side of the shimmering blade before slowly pulling it forward until the blade bit into the material like a knife through butter. Carefully he swung the block to allow the blade to follow one of the marked-out lines. It amazed Victor how quickly and easily Fred had cut out the various shapes which were to become essential parts of corsets when taken upstairs to the sewing machines. He couldn't help blushing when he imagined a lady's undergarment which he didn't understand and far less wanted to think about.

Victor's unwanted thoughts were, at that moment, distracted by the appearance of Norman who had just arrived back from the tea-break which was finished over twenty minutes earlier.

'Always enjoy a good crap at that time of day, you should try it,' the old man yelled in Victor's ear as he passed. On arrival at his jigger, he gave the embarrassed lad a wink, sat at his table and reached up to pull an imaginary handle before making a noise like a steam engine letting off steam. His jigger came into action rather like the rods and pistons on his imaginary engine.

They're all mad here! thought Victor. *What have you done to me, Mum?* At that moment, Tony walked past, on his way to his Band Knife with a trolly load of layered material. *'How's your Fudd?* he shouted above the rumble of Fred's jigger.

'Steaming!' responded Victor, having remembered the required response. *I cannot believe I said that,* thought the lad. *I must be going barmy too.* Satisfied, Tony gave Victor a thumbs-up before heading for his own machine.

So, the morning passed, all the while, Victor watching Fred at work with occasional comments and words of advice. With half an hour still to go before the lunch bell, Fred moved over, inviting Victor to sit in his place. He then produced a clamped layer of off-cut onto which he pencilled a curving line. 'Okay, Vic. Your turn,' he said. 'Just gently guide the material so the blade follows the line. Don't be afraid of it. You'll find you have to swing the block more than you would think, in order to stay on the line.'

With trepidation, Victor sat at the table with eyes glued on the blade. He clutched the block and very carefully slid it behind the blade with one hand before reaching out his other hand to grasp the block on the other side of the blade. Slowly, he pulled the block of material forward until he felt the blade biting in. He was far off the line. Quickly he corrected the direction and found that he was now cutting on the other side of the line.

'Don't over react,' cautioned Fred in his ear. 'Don't worry too much about the line, just get the feel of it as you pull through.'

Victor was sweating and biting the inside of his cheek as he watched that blade slicing through the material, first on one side of the pencil line, then the other. He was improving just as the block came apart in two halves. He had done it!

'Well done! shouted Fred. *'We'll make a cutter out of you, yet! Can you see that red button by your right knee? Give it a tap with your knee.'*

Having done as instructed, the whole assembly of cast-iron and steel blade slowly ground to a standstill. It was only then that Victor noticed that all the other machines were now silent and abandoned as the workers had either walked away to their lunch or, in a few cases, climbed up onto cleared benches with the obvious intention of taking a nap after a quick sandwich.

Following Fred in the direction of the ramp, Victor noticed the girl who had collected him from reception, seemingly so long ago, sitting at her bench with an older couple. They were in deep conversation as they ate their respective lunches.

LINDA

Dorothy was watching Linda closely. Although the girl was talking to them, she noticed that Linda's eyes were following the new boy as he was heading in the direction of despatch for his lunch.

'Do you fancy him?' enquired Dorothy. She was fond of the shy girl who seemed not to have any friends.

'No!' responded the girl indignantly. 'I don't even know him! Anyway, he's got pimples and scruffy ginger hair, and … and … plasters all over him.' Dorothy was amused to see the girl's cheeks changing colour from the usual pearly cream, to pink, then to an amazingly fetching crimson.

VICTOR

Having finished his fish paste sandwiches followed by an apple. Victor, sitting at a bench with Fred, Tony, and Barry, retrieved his pipe from his duffel-bag and proceeded to tamp down the tobacco before applying the lit match. Holding the match to the bowl he sucked several times to draw in the flame. It was somewhat embarrassing when he noticed the gurgle of his own spit left from his previous attempt to get the thing going. He was even more embarrassed when the matchstick flame reached his finger, causing him to yell in pain before jumping to his feet, frantically shaking the blackened and curled stick before sucking his burned fingers.

'Impressive.' said Barry. I had a mate in the Raff who could keep his smelly old pipe going for hours, although he wasn't too popular when he was still puffing like a dragon while we were fuelling up a Lanc. Mind you. I never saw him do a dance like this lad here. What has he got in that instrument anyway? It stinks like my old socks used to when we didn't have time to shower, or bath, or wash, for a month on end. Ah, they were the good old days. Did I ever tell you about …?'

'Yes, you did, Barry,' called out Scabby from the neighbouring bench. 'Many times. Cor … what is that stink?'

'It's 'is pipe!' chipped in Huggy Hen. 'Smells like my old dogs when they've 'ad a swim in the brook.'

Victor, never slow in taking a hint, walked over to his locker and placed the offending article on the shelf, along with the tin of tobacco and matches. He was about to regain his seat when he was suddenly in the plump arms of Huggy Hen. 'There, there,' she said to the startled lad whose chin was propped onto an extremely ample bosom. 'Take no notice of us, we're just 'avin' a lark.' Victor was very much aware of the softness of the bosom while, at the same time, the feel of Huggy Hen's hand tenderly caressing the back of his left ear as though he were a dog.

'Henrietta, would you kindly put that lad down, you don't know where he's been.' To his immense relief and embarrassment, Victor recognised the voice of Bob. 'Okay, you lot, lunch time is over, back to the grind. Fred, how is the lad doing?'

'Getting there, Bob. I'll have him cutting on his own Jigger this afternoon. It's looking dry enough now.'

'Good. I'll come over to see how he's doing later.'

Walking back to his side of the room, Victor glanced over to the bench where he was expecting to see the girl. He was strangely disappointed when he realised, she was not at her bench. Why he should be concerned, he had no idea, or maybe he did if he were to be honest with himself.

Arriving at Fred's jigger, he was greeted with the words, 'Right Vic, you can have a go at starting your own machine. Can you remember how to do it?'

'Yes, I think so,' replied Victor. 'Lever forward, build up the speed then lock the lever.'

'You've got it. I'll stay here and let you do it on your own.'

Victor stepped over to his own Jigger and looked at the table, the cast-iron arm above, and lastly the exposed length of the shining steel blade which was parked on the upstroke and reflecting the afternoon sun. Mindful of the unusual quietness around the room, not to mention several faces pointed in his direction, he stepped into the table recess, grasped the lever, took a deep breath, and pushed it forward. The heavy cast-iron arm immediately went into motion, completing its unfinished upstroke and picking up speed as it thrust the blade down through the slit. All at once, there was an enormous BANG! from under the table, instantly followed by a loud metallic rattling. Victor had disappeared from view.

LINDA

Knowing that she could not bear to watch what she had been warned by Dorothy was about to happen, she had excused herself to go to the lavatory. She was surprised to realise that she cared.

VICTOR

Victor was lying in a foetal position on the floor some ten feet away from his jigger, with his arms over his head and with a racing heart. Realising that he was still alive with two arms, two legs and no pool of blood around him, he raised his head to look around. That's when he saw the sea of grinning faces.

'Okay, mate,' said Fred. 'That was your initiation. You're one of us now, having survived a large balloon tied to the casting under the table, along with lots of empty baked-bean cans. You can get up and take a bow.'

Victor should have been both angry and embarrassed, but instead, felt accepted amongst these mad friendly people, although he suspected they hadn't finished with him yet.

'Okay everyone, you've had your fun, now back to work.' Bob had again come to his rescue.

'Right, Victor,' said Fred. 'Turn your Jigger off. Let's get rid of the rubbish and get your blade out. Time we visited Vernon to get them sharpened.'

Emerging from the doors at the top of the stairs, dismantled blade in hand, Victor tried his best to keep his eyes down as the expected wolf-whistles started. This time, it sounded different, more suggestive? Shyly looking up, he realised it was all aimed at Fred who was beaming down each row of overalled women as he swaggered past. They had not gone very far before Fred stopped to talk to one of the younger women who was working close to the walkway. Victor had no option other to stop and wait. As he stood there, shuffling from one foot to the other and trying not to catch any eyes, that is exactly what he did. A blond girl, five positions down the row in front of him was beckoning him to come over. Any chance of being rescued by Fred evaporated when his conversation with the young woman became more ribald. The girl was still beckoning him to come over as she pointed to something on her machine. Thinking she might have a problem that he may be able to fix, Victor was like a fish on a line, he was hooked and being reeled in. After carefully placing his blade on the floor, and keeping his eyes on the beckoning girl, he eased past the few women separating him from the blond, unaware of the grinning faces of those who could see what was happening. Upon reaching the blond girl who was somewhat older than she had looked from a distance, she enquired, 'What's your name then, sweetheart?'

'Victor.'

'Ooh, that's a posh name, Victor … I like it. Now then, Victor, do you like these?' It was at that moment the startled boy noticed the woman's hand undoing the top of her overalls. In panic, he stumbled back the way he had come, surrounded by shrieks of laughter, and receiving a few pats on his buttocks.

Safely back on the walkway and hurriedly retrieving his blade from the floor, a scarlet faced Victor swept past Fred who immediately followed.

'Blimey, mate. You took your life in your hands back there. Never do that again. Stick to the safety of the walkway. They're like Piranha, they'll gobble you up in seconds. You'll never be seen again … at least, not with your trousers on. It *was* funny though. Your face! It's like a beetroot!'

'Thanks for the warning, but you might have told me first,' said Victor while allowing a faint smile to appear on his blushing face.

'Calm or stormy?'

'Pardon?'

'Vernon wants to know if you want a straight edge or curvy,' said Fred. Turning back to Vernon 'He'll have it straight, like mine.'

Both, watched as Vernon, tucked in his workshop behind a half-door, beavered away on his grinding-wheel, with sparks glittering in the gloomy light. After a few minutes, the elderly man wrapped the two sharpened blades in sheets of oiled paper before handing them back.

Removing a pack of ten Players cigarettes from his pocket, Fred passed it to Vernon as he took the blades. 'Thanks mate. See you later.'

'Is he on Fire-watch tonight?' asked Vernon while nodding in Victor's direction.

'Yep. Though I don't think he's been told yet.'

‘Best let him know then.’ With that comment, Vernon returned to the sewing machine he had previously been repairing.

Turning to Victor as they walked back in the direction of the stairs, Fred commented, ‘You’ll find it’s wise to give Vernon a few fags if you want a really sharp blade, though I doubt he would thank you for a few puffs on that smelly pipe of yours.’

Wary of passing the women, Victor was surprised when not one of them looked up at them as they passed by. Puzzled, he looked around the room until his eyes met those of an older woman, dressed entirely in dark grey, standing in the centre of the room, scowling.

‘Keep going,’ mouthed Fred. ‘That’s Lady Himmler thinking of getting her whip out.’

‘What was that about Fire-watch, Vernon mentioned?’

‘Oh yes, I thought you knew. Mr Dines must have forgotten to tell you during your interview? We have to have someone on the roof till midnight, watching out for any sign of a fire. The material used for corsets is highly flammable and the store can generate heat till all the machines have cooled down. So, someone has to be on lookout. Newbies always have to do that on their first night, after that, you will be on the rota.'

'Well, nobody told me that,' complained Victor. 'What do I do if I see smoke, or something?'

'Oh, you will have a football rattle. You just give it a twirl till the caretaker who lives over the road, blows his whistle to let you know he's heard and phoned for the fire brigade. Then you climb down sharpish, job done.'

LINDA

She was distracted, having watched the new boy leave the room with Fred, she assumed it was to have his blade sharpened. She thought about all those girls up there and wondered if he would be casting his eyes over the pretty ones. She knew that's what boys do, although she had never had a boy looking at her in that way.

'Linda, you're miles away. Your laying-out is all wrong, are you okay?' Dorothy's voice had slowly broken into her thoughts.

'Sorry,' she muttered.

'You're thinking about that boy, aren't you?'

'No!' she protested too loudly.

VICTOR

For the next hour, under Fred's supervision, Victor managed to cut out various blocks of patterns on his own Jigger. He was acutely aware of the times he strayed from the pencilled lines. Just before the afternoon tea-break Bob walked over to check his progress. He closely examined each cut before, to Victor's horror, sweeping the whole lot into the bin alongside the jigger.

'Not bad,' was the only words he said before walking away.

Victor was stunned as he looked at the pink mess in his bin. Meanwhile, Fred had walked over to join him.

'Why did he do that?' asked Victor in disgust. 'I thought he said it wasn't bad.'

'It was a test, mate. It was all old faded material that had been specially prepared for you. The next lot will be real, so you'd better make a good job of it. Come on, the bell's just about to go off.'

As he switched off his jigger, Victor was surprised when the lady who worked with that girl from this morning, appeared at his table. 'Hello, my name's Dorothy, I work over there with Linda. Do you like circuses?' Taken completely aback, Victor replied to the affirmative.

'Well, I just happen to have two tickets to the Mills Circus here in town on Saturday afternoon.' Dorothy was holding the tickets out as she spoke. 'You can have them if you would like to go. Take your girlfriend for a treat.'

'But I haven't got a girlfriend,' replied Victor.

'Oh?' responded Dorothy with a gleam in her eye. 'It just happens that Linda was telling me on Friday, how she would love to go to the circus if only someone would invite her. Are you up for it? You'll find she's rather shy, but once you get to know her, you will realise what a lovely girl she is. It's up to you.'

'Thank you. I'll take them and have a word with her now.' Victor surprised himself with his impetuous boldness.

'Good,' said Dorothy as she handed over the tickets. 'She's in the loo at the moment, she'll be at her bench on her own soon.

I'm going to have a cuppa with my Mike, over there.' She was pointing to the line of Band Knives.

Victor only had a few minutes to wait before he watched the girl approach her bench where she poured herself a drink from a flask. Bucking up his courage and taking a deep breath, he slowly walked over to the girl.

Five minutes later, with a huge grin on his face, Victor entered the despatch area with his head held high, where he immediately opened his locker to retrieve pipe, tobacco and matches. He was a little surprised however, to see fresh tobacco sitting loosely in the bowl of the pipe, not remembering having prepared it earlier. *Oh well,* he thought. *So much going on today, getting forgetful.* Sticking the stem between his lips and striking a match, he held the flame to the bowl and vigorously sucked. *'Yuck! What the hell?'* he yelled spitting out a stream of soapy water to the sound of laughter from around the room.

'You all right, mate?' enquired Fred.

'How's your Fudd? enquired Tony.

'Do you want a nice hug?' enquired Hen.

‘Did that to the bloke who nearly blew up a Lank,’ said Barry.

Scabby picked at another scab on her chin and simply chuckled before flicking something off her fingernail and saying, ‘Blow us some bubbles then.’

‘Got you a mug of tea and an iced bun here, Vic. It’ll take the taste away.’

Victor didn’t know whether to laugh or cry. These people had accepted him, and even better, he never had to smoke that retched smelly old pipe again.

LINDA

‘You’re looking pleased with yourself.’ commented Dorothy when she returned to their bench. ‘Everything all right?’

‘I’ve been invited to the circus,’ replied Linda.

‘Really?’ asked Dorothy. ‘Don’t tell me. It was that new boy.’

‘Yes. How did you guess?’

‘Oh, maybe it was the way you’ve both been trying not to look at each other all day. Plus, I’ve just noticed he’s got the same silly grin on his face the same as you have. I'm so pleased. I'm sure you'll have a great time, you deserve it, luv.'

By the way,' said Linda. 'I asked him if he thinks he's on Fire-watch this evening. When he said he'd just been told by that Fred, I told him it's all a leg-pull. He's ever-so grateful. I like him.'

VICTOR

With his first cutting assignment successfully completed and up to Bob's standard, his duffle-bag, containing his Acceptance Letter but no pipe, tobacco or matches, slung over his shoulder, Victor exited the main door and walked across the car park to retrieve his damaged bicycle from the cycle rack. However, he was shocked to see that it was no longer where he had left it that morning. Glancing across the car park, he saw Fred hurrying in his direction.

'You have to climb that iron ladder over there,' his new friend said while pointing to the side of the building.

'Oh, I don't need to do that,' replied Victor. 'I explained to Mr Dines that I can't do it tonight because of my bike and the fact I hadn't been told. He said not to worry and that he would have a chat with you about it in the morning.'

'Really?' asked Fred with a worried expression now on his face.

'Naa, just kidding, like you've been kidding me all day. Problem is, my bike's been stolen.'

'No, it hasn't, replied Fred with a relieved grin. 'Number seven over there is the caretaker's house. You'll find he's fixed your bike. He does bikes in his spare time. You'll also find his daughter there. The one you've been mooning over all day. Good-night, mate. See you in the morning.

MRS. BUNCE

'Hello Victor, you're just in time for dinner. Did you have a good day?'

'Yes, Mum. Made lots of friends, even got a date for Saturday. Job's okay, but not what I want to do with my life. By the way, I've got this for you to see. It came in the early post this morning.'

Taking the folded envelope, which her son retrieved from his duffle-bag, Mrs. Bunce pulled out the content and exclaimed, 'It says it's from the Shipping Federation, it's a Letter of Appointment to the National Sea Training School. When … how ...?'

'Last month, when you told the head that I wouldn't be staying on. I went to Southampton on my bike, told a kind man in the Cunard Head Office that I wanted to go to sea. He told me to go to The Shipping Federation over the road, I did, and was able to take a medical, pass a simple test-paper and this is the result. You have to sign the consent. Once I'm on a ship, you will be receiving fifty-per-cent of my pay in a monthly allotment. It'll be more than I would be getting from the factory. By the way, Mum?'

'Yes?' asked Victor's bewildered mother.

'How's your Fudd?'

The End

The Pleasure Flight

Terry snaps awake as the sound of approaching voices penetrate his power nap. Checking the wall-clock, the one with narrow aircraft wings pointing to the hours and minutes, he sees that he has been asleep for less than ten minutes.

'She's early,' he mutters as he lifts himself from his office chair. He steps over to the window and peers out across the heads of six approaching figures. He watches a two-seater spitfire lumbering across the field on another of its 'Flight Experiences' as the owner/pilot likes to call them. *What I would give to own one of those* he thinks to himself for the umpteenth time. The group of people have stopped to watch the spitfire which is now lined up for its take-off run. *Three thousand pounds for a twenty-minute flight, lucky sod! A good sort though, never shy when it comes to splashing the cash in the club bar.* Terry steps across to the wall-mirror, an elaborately designed affair with its surface etched with a picture of a spitfire in flight. He checks his neatly trimmed hair to ensure that the wave is still in place. He then runs fingers of both hands along the length of his winged moustache.

'Perfect,' he tells the young man reflected in the mirror. Beneath his coveralls he is wearing cream slacks and a light blue open-necked summer shirt, not that any of these people will see that. He returns to the window as he hears the distinctive throaty roar of the spit' as it begins its roll along the grass runway, just two hundred metres away from his little office. His glance returns to the group of people who are still standing on the spot, clearly excited by the sight of the silver aircraft, now climbing away from the airfield which is returning to its former state of relative quietness, enabling the sound of a hovering skylark to be heard by the discerning ear.

Terry Cunningham, owner of the business named AIRCRAFT RECREATIONAL SERVICES ENTERPRISE which employs one pilot, himself, and owns one aircraft, his de Havilland Tiger Moth bi-plane. Actually, he owns forty-per-cent of the aircraft, as the bank owns the rest of it. The group is once again approaching his office which boasts the company insignia (fortunately not abbreviated as it is on the back of his coverall) and a sign advertising the joy of a Pleasure Flight, during which one can experience the sight of the nearby coast with its stunning cliffs, from the air. *Miss Trimble* Terry recalls. *A half-hour flight, a birthday gift from the family, no doubt.* He examines the approaching group, an elderly couple, a middle-aged couple, a boy about ten years of age, and … *yes!* A beautiful young lady, probably around nineteen or twenty, fair hair falling silkily to her shoulders, slim, honey-brown legs which appear to go on for ever beneath a tight mini-skirt. *My lucky day! Can't wait to be helping Miss Trimble into her parachute! And as for assisting her up onto the wing and over the coaming, into the cockpit ... calm down boyo.* Terry is grinning as he fingers his precious model spitfire which is mounted on his cluttered desk. He adopts a grand pose of importance for the benefit of Miss Trimble when she comes through that door.

The office door opens wide with a clatter. Six people enter, none of them speaks, perhaps a little awed by the various pictures around the walls, each of a different aircraft in flight. Terry is busily filling in forms which do not actually need filling in. He calculates that twenty seconds should be sufficient enough time to establish his importance to this family, particularly Miss Trimble. He eventually looks up and says, 'Good afternoon. How may I help you?'

The middle-aged man steps forward whilst lifting his cap from his slightly balding head 'We've brought Miss Trimble along for her flight.'

'Ah, Miss Trimble, of course. You must forgive me. I was not expecting her for another half hour.'

'Well, we allowed a bit of time for the traffic, do you see? Only there wasn't any … traffic, that is. Isn't that right, our Nel?' He is now addressing the middle-aged lady, presumably his wife.

'That's right Trev, dear,' replies the lady who is moving her head like one of those nodding dogs in the back window of a car. 'Shot straight through like a dose of dia ... salts,'

'We can wait outside if it's not convenient,' says the man. 'I can see you're busy.'

Glancing at the young lady who has removed her sunglasses to peer at him in a studied sort of way, Terry says, 'No. It's fine. We have a few forms for Miss Trimble to sign, then we can get her prepared for her flight.'

'That's very good of you. We appreciate it,' responds the man. 'Isn't that right, our Nel?'

‘Yes, that’s right Trev, dear. Very much appreciated, I’m sure,’ replies the nodding lady.

Addressing himself to the young lady, Terry says, ‘Right then Miss, if you would like to sit here at my desk, I’ll tell you about the thrill you’re about to experience in my capable hands.’

‘Really? You are a smoothy, but in front of my parents and little brother, not to mention my grandparents, I don’t think so,’ replies the girl who is unable, or doesn’t want to stop her eyelashes fluttering.

‘Oh, that’s okay,’ replies Terry. ‘They can sit on the grass outside and watch. It’ll be over in half an hour.’

‘Fast as well as smooth, I like that, Mister ...?’

‘Cunningham … Terry to you.’

‘Is this like the plane I’m going up in?’ It was the old lady who has interjected. She is studying a picture of a Dakota which is mounted on the wall beside the desk, her nose close to the glass.

‘Oh, are you two planning to fly somewhere soon?’ enquires Terry in surprise, while glancing at the old man who is holding on to her elbow.

'No, just me,' replies the old lady. 'It's my birthday present from David and Diane here. Besides, you wouldn't ever get my Walt up in one of those things. He thinks flying's un-natural. Don't you Walter dear.' She is shouting into her husband's left ear at this stage in the conversation.

'So, when is this treat going to happen?' enquires Terry.

'Today, of course, that's why we're here. Never been in one of them things before, though I've seen plenty on the telly. I'm looking forward to one of those trolly dolls, or whatever it is they're called, serving me some Gin.'

'You mean … *You're* Miss Trimble? I thought …' Terry turns to look at the young lady who is in the process of sitting on the corner of his desk and smiling sweetly down at him.

'Oh, you thought it was my granddaughter,' says the old lady with a chuckle. 'No, she's Miss Jenny *Shipton.* They're all Shiptons, except little old me. I kept my maiden name, you see, when me and my Walt married. I didn't want to be named after a jar of fish paste, can't stand the stuff. Do you want to see my passport?'

'What?'

'My passport,' says Miss Trimble as she starts rummaging in her enormous handbag. 'I know you need to show it when going up in one of those things, I've seen it on the telly.'

Terry's day is becoming even more complicated as Miss Shipton slides her bottom along to his side of the desk at the same moment that her little brother is picking up his precious spitfire model and starting to yammer imaginary bullets at him.

'Right, you two. Outside!' It's Mr Shipton coming to his rescue. 'We'll all go outside and leave your grandma with this kind gentleman. Larry, put that plane back on the desk, *carefully!* Pops, you come with us, Grandma will be out soon, then we can all watch her as she reaches for the sky.'

'It's not natural,' mutters the old man as he allows himself to be led by his son to the door. 'Not natural, that's what I say.' The door swings shut behind them, but not before Miss Shipton, the last one out, has turned and peered provocatively over her shoulder at the relieved gentleman who is examining his model spitfire for possible damage. Catching his eye, she asks, 'Mr Cunningham, why have you got the word "arse" printed on the back of your coverall?'

Miss Trimble is tutting as she continues rummaging in her handbag.

'You don't need a passport, Miss Trimble,' says Terry as he places the model back down on the desk. 'We're not leaving the country, just a quick flight along the coast. Now, if you would kindly sign these two forms, here and here where I've pencilled in a cross, I'll fetch you a parachute.'

'A parachute? Why do I need a parachute? We're not even up there yet!'

'Oh, you won't need it, it's simply a precaution we must take in the older aircraft. In any event, you'll need it to sit on.'

'Don't be absurd. Planes have nice comfy seats. I've seen it on the telly.'

'I'll explain when we get out there,' says Terry who is beginning to wish he had not got out of bed this morning. He hands the old lady a biro-pen before reaching into a locker behind the desk from where he retrieves two parachute packs. Having checked that both forms have been graced with a signature he points to a door in the corner of the office and says, 'You may use this room to change into the flying suit you will find in there. Then I'll help you with the chute.'

'Change? I've put on my best frock for this trip, why should I change into a suit? That's not what happens on the telly.'

'Believe me, Miss Trimble, you will be more comfortable, not to mention warmer, in the flying suit.'

'Warmer? Don't you have central heating in your plane?'

Thinking lovingly of the bed he had crawled out of this morning, Terry sighs before replying, 'No central heating, air conditioning, trolly service, film shows or toilets, I'm afraid, so you may want to use the toilets here before going up.'

'Well, this must be a very cheap airline,' complained the old lady. 'Ryanjet have all those things, I've seen …'

'You've seen it on the telly, I know, Miss Trimble. Now if you would like to step into this room, you'll find all you need.'

The inner door opens fifteen minutes later to reveal Miss Trimble looking more like a bottom rung rather than a Top Gun. The flying suit is clearly two sizes too large for her slight figure. 'Very good, Miss Trimble,' says Terry. 'Made to measure. Now let's get you into the parachute harness, step over here if you don't mind.'

'I do mind as it happens,' replies the old lady. 'But if needs must, I suppose I'll have to go along with it. But you won't get me jumping out of your plane, whatever happens.'

'You can be assured; you won't be using the chute for anything other than a seat on this trip. Now if you'd like to stand here with your legs apart, we'll get you sorted.'

'Legs apart? Last time I did that was for Pops, and that was over twenty-five years ago, then it didn't do much good. Just pulling your leg, young man, your face looks fit to scare a scare-crow. Come on then, let's get this over with.'

Together, they step out of the office, both in buff-coloured flying suits, leather helmets, and goggles. Parachute packs are suspended behind their knees thus preventing them from walking normally. The best they can achieve is a waddle like a duck. As they approach the family group, Miss Trimble casts a glare over the group and hisses, 'If I hear a single titter from any of you, I'm going to leave everything to the duck sanctuary.'

This is followed by a burst of laughter from all but Pops who is shaking his head and muttering, 'It's un-natural, we would have been born with wings if we were meant to fly.'

'Right, here we are, Miss Trimble. The de-Havilland DH82 Tiger Moth.'

'What about it?'

'That's the aircraft you're going up in.'

'That thing? It's a big yellow toy!'

'I assure you, Miss Trimble, this is not a toy. One hundred and thirty-seven miles per hour cruising speed.'

'That's fast. I won't allow Trever to go more than forty on the motorway, although I've noticed he sometimes creeps up to fifty. He thinks I don't know. Where's the roof?'

'The what?'

'The roof! It hasn't got a roof. Your plane hasn't got a roof.'

'Oh, I see.' Terry chuckles as he says, 'It's an open cockpit, no roof.'

'What if it rains?'

'You'll be pleased to know the forecast is clear and sunny. Right then, you'll be sitting in the front …'

'I can't drive that thing!'

'I'll be … um … driving, you just sit there and try not to touch anything. Give me your hand, I'll help you up.'

'Where's the door?'

'It doesn't have a door, it's this drop-down flap which I'll lower for you.' Surprisingly, the old lady needs little help to climb onto the lower wing and onto the seat with her parachute pack beneath her. Terry checks her harness then follows suit. He checks his switches as a mechanic from the airfield comes forward to swing the propeller when all is ready. Terry is thankful that further conversation is no longer possible. He notices the spitfire coming in to land before he receives permission from the control tower to taxi out to the runway. Soon he is carefully moving forward. As the nose is higher than his cockpit when the Tiger Moth is on the ground, he must swing from side-to-side in order to see what is ahead. He wonders what Miss Trimble will have to say about his erratic steering when they eventually land.

In no time, he has the Tiger Moth trimmed at two-thousand feet following a seamless take-off. Soon they are flying above the sea with the cliffs off to their right. Up till this point, Miss Trimble's head has been moving around to take in the view, when suddenly she throws both arms into the air as though she is on a roller-coaster. Terry is certain that he hears her shout with joy. He decides to put the aircraft into a dive to see how she reacts. With the slipstream whistling in their muffled ears the old lady is pumping her arms in excitement. He is unable to resist it as he shouts, 'Right then, Miss Trimble, see how you like this.' He puts the Tiger Moth into a loop. Her arms are still in the air. Another loop … arms still in the air, both thumbs raised. A roll followed by a barrel-roll. Miss Trimble, with both arms still in the air, is clapping her hands, she is *loving* it!

All too soon, it's time to return to the airfield. A neat three-point landing ends Miss Trimble's half-hour pleasure flight. The old lady is out on the wing before the propellor stops spinning. She had not used the drop-down door but simply cocked her leg over the coaming. As her family approaches the parked Tiger Moth she nimbly steps down from the wing and waddles over to the group to embrace her husband. Having exited the Tiger Moth,

Terry stands on the grass and watches the excited group for a moment before approaching. Miss Trimble is the first to notice his waddling approach and turns to face him, a huge grin plastered on her face.

'That was amazing, young man. I loved every minute, especially the aerobatics. Now, I have a confession to make. I have been stringing you along the whole time. I am an addictive thrill junky. It was water skiing last month and I'm booked for zorbing with my WI group next month. Now, get me out of this outfit and you can join us for a beer in that pub over the road. I get the feeling our Jenny would like to get to know you better.'

The End

Ruffy

The journey back to Thomas and Emma's home in Kirby would take most of the daylight hours. They had set out soon after a breakfast of mutton pie, which the Inn-keeper's rotund wife had proudly set before them, following their appearance in the lounge that morning.

'Now, you get tucked into this while my Jack fetches you a tankard of beer from the barrel. You've a long journey ahead of you,' she stated unnecessarily, 'and you'll be needin' some sustenance to keep you warm. The lad's feedin' your 'orse at this moment, and 'e'll get it 'arnessed to your trap in time for you to leave. And don't you worry about your trunk, our Jack'll bring it down and get it stowed.'

Emma's stomach had unfortunately rebelled after the first tentative sample of the pie, although Thomas had managed his own with relish. 'Are you quite well, my dear?' he had enquired as he watched his wife pushing the platter away with a slight shudder.

‘Yes, I am well enough thank you Thomas. I have no appetite this morning, that’s all. Thank you for your concern. After what the doctor said, I feel as though I have let you down. I know how much you wanted a son.’

Now, having left several milestones behind them along the lane leading from the city, they had passed through a scattering of fields yet to be harvested, some dense woods and a few hamlets of thatched cottages, the young couple were sitting wordlessly side-by-side behind the trotting horse to the sound of the rumbling wheels, each in their own thoughts. Thomas, the heir to a modest estate following the demise of his father, now concerned for the future of the property with no son to take it on. Emma wondering what the shocking news of her inability to bear a child, following her riding accident, would do to their marriage. They had been newly-weds just eighteen months ago. The accident had occurred just three months into their marriage while following the chase across open fields which were surrounded by gated hedges. At first, the injuries seemed superficial, but as each month had passed, expectation of a pregnancy dissolved into disappointment. The estate had been in the family for several hundred years and Thomas had expected to pass it on to future generations. Finally, at Thomas's suggestion, Emma had agreed to allow the city doctor to examine her, and now they knew. No children, no heir.

As morning extended into early afternoon, Emma, not having eaten a morsel so far that day noticed the slight discomfort of hunger and the need to partake of food. Removing her melancholy gaze from the nodding head of the trotting horse, she turned to Thomas before saying, 'Thomas, would it be convenient to stop for a while? I'm aware that the landlady kindly prepared a packed lunch and I feel I could now eat something, so long as it isn't cold mutton pie.'

'Forgive me my dear. I was lost in contemplation and had not noticed the passage of time. Of course, we can stop for a while to comfort our needs. If I recall, beyond this slight rise we happen to be climbing, there is a grand stopping point where there happens to be a modest pond hidden by gorse. That should serve every purpose I should not wonder.'

Five minutes later, while Thomas hobbled, fed, and watered the horse, Emma had busied herself with the spreading of a travelling rug and the unpacking of the hamper which had been prepared by the landlady. She had been relieved to discover that the pie of generous proportions, which she found beneath the loaf of freshly baked bread and a side of ham, was one of apple and blackberry. Her spirits were slightly lifted with the generosity of the fare provided by the landlady, particularly as she watched Thomas tucking in with relish.

Although the couple had not previously noticed the ducks on the pond when they had first arrived at this perfect spot, the ducks had noticed them and lost no time in responding to the possibility of food being offered. With a great deal of quacking and expectation they arrived at the picnic spot and clustered around the blanket, one even bold enough to step onto the corner of the material. With much amusement at the comical antics of the colourful birds, any remaining tension between husband and wife was slowly dissipated as laughter accompanied the shared meal.

After declining a second portion of pie, Emma sat back, with her elbows resting on the blanket behind her. There, she gazed up into the branches of a silver birch which had been offering welcome shade. She momentarily listened to the twittering of a hovering skylark which had previously gone un-noticed. She became aware of the movement of her husband as he shook the crumbs from their plates onto the grass, to the frantic shoving and shovelling of their new feathered friends. As relative quietness eventually replaced the quacking, Emma asked, 'Thomas, can you ever forgive me? I know what this means to you and how much you wanted a son. It is all my fault. I should never have taken that hedge on the gallop, it was so …'

'My darling girl,' interrupted Thomas. 'It was me who encouraged you, if you cast your mind back. I insisted that you join the hunt and it was I who led you to that boundary hedge. If we are looking for fault, it all rests with me. What is most important to me now my sweet, is your physical and mental health.'

'But the future of the estate! You are bound to …'

'I've been thinking about that,' replied Thomas. I have a cousin in Kent who I believe has children, my closest surviving relative. It's been many a year since I last saw Bernard and his wife Felicity, although we have remained in touch by occasional correspondence. We will have to invite them over to stay, in order to become more familiar with them. It has been my intention for you to meet him and his family for some time now. Perhaps a time will come when their son will be able to inherit. He is no older than six years at the moment, I imagine.' Thus saying, Thomas continued packing the picnic hamper, his facial expression not giving away his innermost thoughts.

Becoming aware of her need, with a little embarrassment, Emma quietly said,’ If you’ll excuse me, dear husband, I need to leave for a moment to discover a secluded spot amongst the gorse. I will not go beyond calling distance.’

‘Very well, my dear. I shall stow the hamper and harness Jessy to the trap. Plenty of time, no hurry.’

It was as Thomas was swatting away an inquisitive wasp, whilst harnessing the horse, that the quietness was split by a piercing scream. In consternation he ran in the direction of where he had last seen Emma as she had entered the gorse. *‘Emma? I’m coming! Where are you?’* he called as he pushed through the gorse clumps.

‘Over here. Oh my God! Come quickly! It’s a baby. It’s dead!’

Pushing through the dense gorse, Thomas swept into a clearing where he was confronted with the sight of his wife standing rigidly in the centre, both hands to her mouth. *‘Where is it?’* he demanded.

Running into his outstretched arms, she pointed in the general direction of the opposite side of the clearing, saying. 'Oh, Thomas! It's over there ... in a ditch under some gorse. It's dirty, and covered in sheep wool.'

'Go back to the horse and trap, my dear. I'll take a look and see what is to be done.'

Silently, Emma obeyed her husband. She was still shaking as she held the harness while calming the horse, although it was the gentle nuzzling of Jessy that had the calming effect on herself. A few minutes later, Thomas reappeared and to Emma's horror, he was holding the baby in his arms. 'Don't show me!' she hurriedly said. 'Wrap it in the picnic blanket. I do not want to see its face.'

Walking directly toward her with a huge grin on his face, Thomas called, *'It's a stuffed toy, some sort of animal, possibly a bear!'*

'A bear?' enquired Emma. 'How on earth did it get there?'

'It was deliberately left there, presumably by a child,' answered Thomas. 'There's a note in what looks like a child's hand. It was tucked into a tear on its back. Difficult to make out the words as the paper is quite damp. I can just make out the word *needd* and something that looks like *bruv.'*

'Let me see,' said Emma, whilst reaching for the paper. 'Something something need could be *needed* do you think? Something something br something v something … that could be *brave.* I cannot make out the next line. The last line could be something something something la something br something j orf something n something something g. That is all I can make of it, I'm afraid,' she said as she handed the damp piece of paper back to Thomas. As she did so, she took the toy from his other hand and proceeded to examine it. 'It does rather resemble a bear, doesn't it?' Peering more closely, she said, 'I do not think the back of it *is* torn, it looks more like a deliberate cut to me. Someone, possibly a child, has deliberately made that slit, in which to hide the note. Oh, I wish we could manage to read it. It must have been important to the child, whoever he or she is,' she continued in frustration.

After a further re-examination of the note, Thomas remarked, 'This final word, orf..n..g could be a child's attempt to write *orphanage.'*

'Let me see?' said Emma excitedly. 'Yes, you could be right. What is in front of that word? La.br.j. *It's Laybridge! It must be. Laybridge Orphanage!'*

'Is there an orphanage in Laybridge?' wondered Thomas. 'I've not heard of one.' In any event, this is nothing to do with us. Come along, we must be on our way if we are to get home before sunset.'

Over the following weeks, Emma distracted herself by remaining busy with her garden, as well as visiting local families, usually to take food which had resulted from her garden harvesting. She was also head of the church flower arranging team, a task she loved and performed diligently.

Meanwhile, Thomas remained busy with the running of the estate and meetings with the tenant farmers. Nothing further was spoken between husband and wife about the devastating news each was trying to come to terms with.

Emma, an only child, had grown up in a world devoid of the company and friendship of other children in a remote part of the Yorkshire Dales where her father owned land for grazing sheep.

Since her mother had died, when Emma was at an early age, she had yearned for a sister, someone to confide in and with whom she could enjoy feminine pursuits such as flower arranging, dressmaking, painting and craft. For this reason, she had always imagined the possibility of having a daughter, after having produced an heir for Thomas. As far as she was aware, Thomas had yet to write to his cousin in Kent, for surely, he would have consulted her about the necessary arrangements for a visit.

One wet morning in late September, when the weather did not allow outside pursuits in the garden, Emma found herself in one of the third-floor rooms which was basically used as a walk-in-cupboard for the storing of furniture and objects brought out with the changing of the seasons. Here she came across an oak chest in which Thomas kept oddments he no longer needed or used, but which he was loath to discard, or give away. She was aware that no secrets were kept in the chest as he had once encouraged her to look through the items contained within, in case any should be of interest or use to her. She therefore had no hesitation on this wet morning to lift the lid and peer into the interior. She was however, unprepared for the shock of seeing, lying on the top of the general contents, the toy bear looking up at her with it's one remaining eye. Emma gasped and quickly stepped back, aware of the mad beating of her heart. The bear had completely escaped her mind. In fact, she was not even aware that Thomas had brought it home with them on that sunny day all those weeks ago.

Not having the heart to close the heavy lid over the bear, Emma turned for the door and left the room. Her heart was still beating rapidly as she descended the stairs where, by chance Mrs Lefroy the housekeeper happened to be ascending, 'Are you quite well Madam?' asked the housekeeper. 'You're looking pale, and if I may be so bold as to say, a bit shaken up.'

'Oh, Mrs Lefroy,' replied Emma who had not noticed the housekeeper until nearly on top of her, 'Thank you for enquiring, I am very well, just a little tired I think. Tell me, do you happen to know if there is an orphanage, or child's home in Laybridge?'

'Strange you should ask, Madam. The Master asked me the same thing weeks ago. As I told him, yes there is such an establishment in Laybridge. It's opposite St Mary's Convent at the lower end of River Street.'

'Thank you, Mrs Lefroy. Just wondering. That will be all, thank you.'

It was during dinner that evening that Emma brought up the subject of the orphanage. ‘Thomas dear, did you think any more about writing to your cousin?’

Laying down his soup spoon, her husband hesitated for a moment before replying, ‘As a matter of fact, my dear, in answer to your question, I have not done so as yet.’

‘Oh, I see. I only ask because I know how important succession is to you. Is it still your intention to communicate with him at some point?’

‘Well, I’ve been thinking about that for some time. Perhaps it would be better not to rush into things before we have considered all possibilities.’

‘I understand, Thomas, but you heard what the specialist had to say. I’m unable to bear you a child. It breaks my heart to have to repeat it but it would appear that it will not be possible for us to have children of our own.’

‘Ah … perhaps there can be another way.’

‘Another way?’ repeated Emma as she sipped more soup from the edge of her spoon before laying it down and dabbing her lips with her napkin. 'What other way might there be?' she enquired with raised eyebrows.

'Adoption.'

'Adoption? Would that involve a visit to River Street in Laybridge by any chance,' she asked with a smile on her lips.

'How do you …'

'I found the bear today, in your chest.'

'Oh … What do you think, my love? Might be worth considering?'

'I've been considering it all day, dearest of husbands. I think we should go, and we should take that bear with us.'

'You mean …?'

'Yes, adoption could be the answer.' Emma could no longer restrain herself as she arose to step around the table where she knelt by her husband's chair to take his hand. 'Oh Thomas, wouldn't it be wonderful to hear the sounds of children in this house, to bring them up ourselves, to teach them …to … love them?'

'Them? How many are you thinking of, my dear?'

'Twelve, sixteen, does it matter?'

'Well, I propose that we investigate the possibility of just one for the time being, to see how it goes. It would be a huge life-changing commitment. Perhaps there will be a suitable boy waiting for a home, who knows.'

'A boy? Yes, of course,' replied Emma, deciding not to push too far at this stage. 'When shall we go to Laybridge?'

'I will write to them first, also to our legal representative to establish procedures in these matters. Then we shall see.'

'That's wonderful,' said Emma before kissing her husband's hand and holding it against her cheek. 'I do hope we shall not have to wait too long before we can visit the orphans. I wonder if we will be able to find the child who left that message in the bear?'

'Well, I suggest you don't lift your hopes too high at this time, my dear,' replied Thomas. 'Let us first establish the protocol for this situation. We must not risk disappointment with your state of mind being as it has these last weeks.'

'I understand, darling husband, and I'm sorry if I have been somewhat withdrawn. I did not intend to cause you undue concern, for I know you also have been bitterly disappointed. Having once again seen that toy, I am unable to get the child who left that message out of my mind these recent hours. Don't you think it might have been intended that we should be the people who found it? Such strange things have been known to happen.'

Arising from his chair, Thomas gently lifted Emma from her knees and took her into his arms where he enfolded her into a firm embrace. 'Yes, it's possible I suppose, but highly unlikely.'

'Excuse me master. Shall I clear the soup dishes and bring in the main course?' Thomas quickly released his wife, both laughing as he answered the maid, 'Yes Primrose, forgive us, we had not heard you enter. Please do as you suggested.'

The girl grinned as she caught Emma's eyes which were showing a hint of the old sparkle that used to be there in happier times.

With the meal over, Thomas dabbed his lips and moustache with his napkin which he folded onto the plate before saying, 'Now, let me go to my study, I have some letters to write. I will join you in the parlour shortly.'

It was three long weeks before Thomas was able to draw the trap to a stop at the gates of the orphanage in Laybridge. Stepping down onto the cobbled road, he looked through the bars of the locked gates. The site of the grim two-storied flat-fronted building gave him no reassurance of the manner in which the incarcerated children were housed. He noticed several children of varying ages working in the vegetable gardens which bordered a short drive. All were dressed in filthy rags.

'What can you see?' enquired Emma who was still seated on the trap while holding the reins.

'The house, my dear. Also, a number of children working in the grounds.'

'Can I 'elp you?' A tall thin man dressed in a scuffed grey suit which had clearly seen better days had appeared as if from nowhere. He approached from the other side of the gate, and allowed his gaze to take in the couple and the horse and trap.

'I, that is, *we*, have an appointment to see Mrs Rimble.'

'I see,' replied the unsmiling man. 'Would you 'appen to be Mr Heaverly by chance?'

'Mr and Mrs Everly. We are half an hour before our appointed time but I am sure you will understand the vagaries of travel. Perhaps you would kindly open the gate and arrange for someone to tend to the horse whilst we take refreshment?'

'She didn't say anyfing about lookin' after an 'orse,' mumbled the man as he produced a previously hidden keyring from beneath his jacket. 'Tek it up to the building next to the 'ouse. I'll get it sorted. Watch out none of them brats try to climb on as you pass them.'

A moment later, as Thomas was handing Emma down from the trap, an over-dressed lady approached from the direction of the front door of the house. 'Mr and Mrs Everly,' she exclaimed in a high-pitched voice. 'How kind of you to be so punctual. Do leave your horse and cart here, Jethro will take care of them.' She gave the thin man a warning look as she spoke. She continued with an air of importance 'Now, please come into my office, if you would be so kind. I will arrange refreshments for you after your long journey.'

Following the woman who was clearly Mrs Rimble, although she had omitted to introduce herself, Emma noticed that all the children in the garden had stopped whatever they were doing in order to stare at them.

'Are these all the children?' she enquired of the back of the woman.

Turning, Mrs Rimble replied, 'Oh, no. There are many more inside. They will be working at various crafts such as basket making, rug latching, embroidery, lace making, that kind of thing.'

'When do they play?' enquired Emma.

'Oh, they don't have time to play.' answered the woman. 'No, it'll be supper and bed at sunset.'

Once seated on a sofa in a comfortably furnished lounge, which also clearly served as an office, Mrs Rimble pulled a cord by the fireplace and asked, 'Would you like tea and sandwiches before we get down to business?'

Before either had time to answer, a knock on the door proceeded the entry of a thin girl of around twelve years of age. 'Ah, Rosette, kindly fetch the tea-trolly we prepared earlier,' ordered Mrs Rimble. After the girl had curtsied and departed, the lady said, 'One of our older girls, soon to go into service as a scullery maid.'

'Is that what happens to those who are not adopted?' asked Emma in shock.

'Would you rather they were flung out onto the street?' responded the woman while lifting her eyebrows. 'Girls into service or one of the mills, boys into labour of some kind, such as coalmines, sweeps, and such like. Some into the army or navy, all glad to have them. Now then, in your correspondence, Mr Everly, you say that you're interested in the possibility of adopting a boy. What sort of age were you thinking? We have them from unwanted babies up to thirteen.'

'Before we talk about that,' chipped in Emma as she reached into her bag, 'May I ask if you have ever seen this toy bear? At least we think it is supposed to be a bear.'

'Let me see,' responded the woman as she reached across the coffee table that separated them. Following an all too brief examination, the woman sniffed and said, 'No, I cannot say I have. Why do you ask?'

'We found …' Emma lapsed into silence as Thomas gently squeezed her arm. At that moment a knock on the door proceeded the entrance of Rosetta with the afore mentioned tea trolly which she pushed over to the side of the coffee table. As she did so, the girl let out a startled breath and gasped, 'That's Ruffy, Clemmy's bear. She lost it, that day some of the younger children were taken into the countryside by the nuns in those carts.'

'Remarkable!' said Mrs Rimble. 'I'll see that it's returned to her if you would kindly leave it with me.'

'No!' said Emma sharply. 'I would like to meet her and return the bear myself. Please arrange it … now.'

'As you wish,' replied Mrs Rimble indifferently. I'll take you to see her, you may also come across other children you would like to meet. Rosetta, do you know where Clemmy is at the moment?'

'She's working in the laundry, Mrs Rimble,' replied the girl.

'In the laundry? Oh no, I don't think we would want to go down there,' said the woman with a slight shudder. 'Go and fetch her, Rosetta, while these kind folk enjoy some refreshments. Make sure she's presentable, mind.'

'No!' interrupted Thomas. 'We will go with Rosetta, perhaps you would like to remain here and prepare whatever paperwork our legal representative will need to examine. We will be taking the child with us.'

'But you haven't met …'

'I think we have, possibly in a way you will never understand,' replied Thomas. Taking his wife's hand, he smiled at her and said, 'Emma? Shall we?'

Mrs Rimble was still seated at the coffee table with a puzzled look on her face as Thomas and Emma followed the twelve-year-old girl out of the room.

'The laundry is down in the cellar,' Rose explained. 'We will pass other workshops at this level as we go through to the stairs. Would you like to look at the girls in those as we pass?'

'Perhaps not,' replied Thomas. 'We saw some boys outside as we came in. Are there any others?'

'Yes, as well as those you saw, some of the older boys are working with the animals at the back. We have chickens, pigs and three milking cows.'

'Thank you, Rose, we will be wanting to meet the boys later, but first things first, let's go and find Clemmy.'

'You will like her, she's ...special.'

'Really?' said Emma. 'In what way is she special?'

'I dunno,' replied the girl. 'Just ... special.'

As the three of them, led by Rosetta, walked along several corridors they passed various workshops where the couple could see girls of all ages working industrially under the supervision of members of staff. This all gave Thomas the impression of a factory, rather than a home. 'Where do the children sleep?' he asked Rosetta, having just peered into a room where he could see some girls working with cane on some old chairs and screens.

'The dormitories are upstairs, girls at one end, boys at the other. The boys have beds to themselves but the girls mostly have to double-up as there are more of us. The boys are taken faster than the girls as they are considered more useful for farming and building, that kind of stuff. Here we are, we need go down these stairs.'

At the foot of the stone stairs was a closed door which Rosetta opened for the couple. The scene and accompanying smell of ammonia, and something else she couldn't identify, momentarily took Emma's breath away as she entered the room ahead of her husband. On one side was a line of butler sinks, each with a girl leaning over the rim working away with a scrubbing brushes and washboards. Emma noticed that their pinnies were wet through and that their hands were red raw. A long table on the opposite wall contained numerous wicker baskets, each containing a variety of clothing and bedding. At the far end of the room was a drying area. There, she could see several girls using flat-irons which were clearly heated by a stove. One or two girls stopped working to glance at the visitors. Their eyes were dull. Each was wearing a bonnet which failed to hide lank hair, some halfway down to their waists. There were no windows and what little light the room had was filtered from a line of dirty skylights where the external wall met the exposed brick ceiling.

Letting out her breath, Emma looked up into her husband's eyes to see that he was equally appalled by the conditions in which these girls were working. Meanwhile, Rosetta had entered the room behind them and had spoken to one of the girls who was sorting through the contents of one of the baskets. She returned to the couple and said, 'Clemmy's outside helping with the sheets.

It's this way.' She turned to lead them to a door they hadn't previously noticed which was at the far end of the room alongside the stove and boiler. Many eyes followed them as they passed through the hot fetid room. To their instant relief, they were soon in the refreshing air where several girls were to be seen hanging out sheets with the use of wooden pegs.

'That's Clemmy,' said Rosetta while pointing to a small girl who was industrially running to and frow, fetching sheets from the baskets to take them to the taller girls who were doing the pegging. She was dressed in the same drab brown pinafore dress as the others, only hers was two sizes too large for her. Beneath her bonnet could be seen golden hair which tumbled down her back. There was no smile, just a blank expression of sadness. Without hesitation, Emma stepped in the direction of the little girl while at the same time, removing the bear which had been previously returned to her bag. Becoming aware of the strange adult approaching her, the girl stopped running and looked up into the kindest smiling face she had ever seen. It was then that she noticed the bear held in the lady's outstretched hand.

'My Ruffy! It's my Ruffy! You found my Ruffy,' she cried as she reached out for her toy bear. *'I knew you would! I knew if I left*

him, you would find me.' The girl was now crying sweet tears as she hugged the bear to her little chest. She took her wet eyes from the one-eyed bear and looked up to search Emma's face which also had tears streaming down her cheeks. 'Have you come to take us?' she asked through trembling lips.

'Yes,' whispered Emma, for at that moment she was unable to find her voice. 'If that's what you want.'

'Oh yes please!' replied the girl. 'Ruffy says he wants us to go with you, but … but …' The girl was unable to finish what she was about to say.

By this time Rosetta and Thomas had quietly joined them. 'Clemmy has an older brother here with her,' explained Rosetta. 'They are afraid they will be parted. Clemmy is only five and David is twelve, the same as me. She won't go without David if she has any choice.'

'Rose, you won't let them split us up, will you?' pleaded Clemmy. 'You promised.'

'Where is the boy?' asked Thomas gruffly.

'He'll be working with the pigs, most like,' replied Rosetta. 'He loves those animals almost as much as he loves Clemmy, but in a different way. I'll take you to him.'

'We'll all go together,' replied Thomas. 'Lead the way please.'

Rosetta stepped ahead of the others to be quickly joined by Clemmy who immediately grasped the older girl's hand. Soon they were approaching the pigsty where they leaned over the wall to see the boy who was busily scratching the neck of a large sow.

'David, I've brought these gentle-folk over to see you,' said Rosetta.

'They found my Ruffy,' butted in Clammy.

'Son,' said Thomas. 'I see you love animals.'

'Yes, sir. I do, right enough.'

'Right then, you'll be coming home with us,'

Getting to his feet, the boy glumly said, 'You want me to work on your farm. I knew it would happen sooner or later, we're to be split up then.'

'Not at all,' replied Thomas, 'You are both coming. With your agreement, we want to give you a permanent home with a view to adoption. How does that sound?'

'Did you hear that, Clemmy? They want us both!'

'Of course they do, silly,' retorted Clemmy. 'Ruffy chose them to be our new mummy and daddy, who's a clever bear then?' the girl said as she kissed the bear's nose.

'I'll leave you all now,' said Rosetta quietly. 'You'll be wanting to return to the office, David will take you. Don't forget to take those muddy boots off, David' With that, the girl turned and ran back to the house.

'She's a nice girl,' said Emma, addressing the two children. 'She seems to be very fond of you both.'

'She's looked after us ever since we arrived,' replied Clemmy.

'Our mother died giving birth to Clemmy.' added David. 'Dad couldn't cope with working and looking after us, so he put us in this home a few months later. We've been told that he died of TB a couple of years later. Rose took us in hand, showed us the best way to stay out of trouble and became like a mother to Clemmy, even though she was only seven years old herself. We'll miss her.'

Five minutes later, all four of them were seated in the office which seemed another world after all that Thomas and Emma had just witnessed.

'So, you've decided to take both David and Clementine,' said Mrs Rimble who was now seated at her desk. 'That's for the best, I think. They are very close, you know.' I have Clementine's papers prepared; you will excuse me while I do the same for David. I've looked through the documents your legal representative prepared and all seems satisfactory. I will, of course, need to notify the local magistrate's office of the arrangement. The financial settlement is most acceptable. Thank you. I assume you will be wanting to take the children immediately?'

'Absolutely,' replied Emma. Will you be kind enough to allow them to go and collect any of their possessions they would like to bring with them.'

'They do not have any personal possessions other than a toy. It is not allowed,' replied Mrs Rimble with a sniff.

'Well then,' said Thomas. 'If you would be so kind as to complete David's papers, we'll be on our way.'

Throughout this conversation, the two children had quietly sat on the sofa between the two adults who were to become their parents. Clemmy was happy to lean against Emma who was gently squeezing her hand. The bear was quite content to be resting in Clemmy's arm, its one eye seeming to be looking up at Emma in approval.

The afternoon sun continued to shine as the horse and trap with its four passengers passed the last house on the edge of the town, the open countryside stretched out before the trotting horse. The youngest person on board was unable to stop voicing her wonder at all that she was seeing, trees, flowers, sheep, distant hills, fluffy clouds, birds in the air or in the branches. It was all so beautiful to her young mind. Meanwhile, David, sitting alongside Thomas, was thrilled when allowed to take the reins and guide Jessy along the lanes. There was much laughter and giggling between the two excited children, although the grown-ups both seemed to be preoccupied in their thoughts.

A mile or so beyond the town limits Emma called to her husband, 'Thomas? Are you thinking what I am thinking, by any chance?'

'I believe so,' replied Thomas. At that moment, he made up his mind. 'This is a mistake. We're going back. Hand me the reins, David.' A moment later, Thomas was easing the horse and trap around on the narrow lane.

'What's happening?' asked Clemmy. 'Why are we going back? Don't you want us anymore? Did we do something wrong?'

'Oh, sweetheart,' replied Emma, giving the girl a firm hug. We want you very much, but we are going back for Rose. We can see what she means to you both, and we want her also, to belong in our family. The five of us together, and Ruffy, of course.'

The End

Other books written by Paul Ludford and now available.

DON'T TAKE A LOOK

A novel set during World War One, featuring a family who own and run a horse-drawn narrowboat plying trade on the Basingstoke Canal. A stranger who comes into their midst will change their lives forever.

IMAGINATION

Paul's first book of short stories.

Featuring 40 tales, each the product of his wide imagination.

At the time of this publication, Paul has completed three additional books which are due to be published.

For additional information,

or to purchase currently available books, go to

www.paulludford.com

I hope you enjoyed IMAGINATION 2 as much as I enjoyed writing each of these short stories as ideas popped into my head. It has been fun, particularly as I seldom know where the stories are going until the characters take control of my fingers on the keyboard. This often results in surprise and laughter on my part, even a tear or two.

I would like to thank my long-suffering wife Margaret who always knows when to leave me alone with my keyboard, and who is a loyal and wise critic. She has always been so generous with her encouragement.

I would also like to thank Reg Talbot, the retired railway gatekeeper who inspired my story; THE GATEKEEPER.

I should also mention Theresa Loosley of Biddles Ltd. She has always been so helpful in the publication of my books, particularly with the design of the covers. I am so grateful.

Paul Ludford